Other titles by

LILIAN PEAKE
IN HARLEQUIN PRESENTS

Other titles by

LILIAN PEAKE
IN HARLEQUIN ROMANCES

Many of these titles and other titles in the
Harlequin Romances series are available at your
local bookseller or through the Harlequin Reader
Service. For a free catalogue listing all available
Harlequin Presents and Harlequin Romances,
send your name and address to:

HARLEQUIN READER SERVICE,
M.P.O. Box 707
Niagara Falls, N.Y. 14302

Canadian address:
Stratford, Ontario, Canada N5A 6W4.
or use order coupon at back of book.

LILIAN PEAKE

no friend of mine

Harlequin Books

TORONTO • LONDON • NEW YORK • AMSTERDAM • SYDNEY • WINNIPEG

Harlequin Presents edition published July 1977
ISBN 0-373-70698-7

Original hardcover edition published in 1972
by Mills & Boon Limited

Printed in Canada

Woodman, spare that tree!
    Touch not a single bough!
In youth it sheltered me,
    And I'll protect it now.

GEORGE POPE MORRIS, 1802–1867.

CHAPTER I

IT was Saturday and the town clock chimed half-past mid-day. The people hurrying past the shop were too pre-occupied with thoughts of lunch to hover and gaze as they usually did at the radios and televisions and electrical equipment on display in the window.

Elise tugged her handbag from underneath the counter and opened the door into the office at the back of the shop. Her employer, Phil Pollard, was at his desk checking invoices against goods received.

He glanced up, his round boyish face with its smooth cheeks and high colour crinkling characteristically into a smile.

'Going home?'

Elise nodded, thinking he looked younger than his years despite his thickening figure, and she knew that where she, his part-time assistant, was concerned, he traded on the fact. He had never given up hope that one day he would persuade her to marry him.

He lifted his hand, still holding a batch of invoices. 'Right, see you Monday. Enjoy your weekend. Doing anything special?'

His tone was light, but the touch of wistfulness which underlined it was not lost on Elise. His constant dread, he had told her once, half in fun, was that she would arrive at work one day wearing an engagement ring. But Elise knew that the chances of that happening were as likely as a snow-storm at the Equator.

Answering his question, she shook her head. 'Just lazing —after I've done the household chores and talked Dad and my brother into tidying up.'

'Well,' she could see his mind had already flitted back to

7

his work, 'if you're at a loose end, just ring me. We could go for a run in the car.' He smiled hopefully as if thinking that perhaps this time she might take him up on his invitation.

She closed the shop door behind her, cutting off sharply the buzz of the warning bell. She lingered for a few moments to inspect with pride the window display which she had arranged, avoiding with something like distaste her own reflection which stared transparently back at her from the plate glass window.

She never looked at herself for long. Her clothes were plain, her hair shoulder-length, its colour a non-committal light brown. She took little care with her appearance. 'I've no one to dress up for,' she would tell herself whenever a feeling of dissatisfaction prodded her sleeping conscience into wakefulness. She closed her mind, locked and bolted it, to the awareness of the passing of time and to the misgivings which nagged at her whenever she saw girls five or six years her junior comfortably settled with husbands and the beginnings of a family.

As she stared through herself at the window display, she allowed her eyes to be caught and held by the stereo receiver she longed to buy. If only, she thought, turning away and walking to the bus stop, I could persuade Dad to let me install it in the sitting-room. For months she had tried to make him change his mind, but he was adamant.

As she waited in the queue and counted out her fare, she could almost hear her father's voice. 'It's out of the question, love. You know how much work I have to do at home, marking students' homework and preparing lectures. I couldn't stand the noise.'

The bus stopped and the people filed on. She paid her fare and gazed out of the window. She supposed he was right. His work at the technical college had to come first and now he was a widower, he seemed to live for little else, apart from his garden.

She walked along the driveway, taking out her door key and passing her brother's car which was parked as usual in front of the garage. She opened the door, hoping that one of the men had set the table for lunch.

The warmth of the central heating came at her as she entered the hall. It was not a modern house they lived in, yet not so old that it could not be so described by an estate agent if they ever decided to move.

As she hung up her coat, she half-listened to the raised voices coming from the sitting-room. There was nothing unusual about that, as her father and brother often argued. Then she listened more carefully. Surely there was a third voice, a man's, pleasing, self-assured and talking as familiarly and easily as if he were among friends?

'Elise!' She heard her brother calling. With an anxious gesture she raised her hands to smooth her hair and opened the sitting-room door. Three pairs of eyes turned towards her—her father's, her brother's and those of a stranger.

He was tall, his face fine-boned and sensitive, and his deepset keenly blue eyes, which were now warm and smiling, gave advance warning of a temperament which could be a force to be reckoned with if crossed. His manner was relaxed and he was looking at her as if he had known her all his life.

'Hallo, Elise,' he said. 'Remember me?'

She stared, searched his face for a clue to his identity, groped about bewildered in the dark corners of her memory and stumbled on the answer.

'You're not—you're not Lester Kings?'

'He is,' answered her brother. 'It took you long enough to recognise him.'

'She could be forgiven for that, Roland,' her father said. 'It is, after all, let me see, seventeen years since she last saw him. That's right, isn't it, Lester?'

'Quite right, Mr. Lennan. She was—er—nine.' He raised an eyebrow. 'Correct, Elise?'

9

'Yes. And you and Roland were—to me—"old men" of seventeen!'

Lester laughed and moved towards her, hand outstretched. 'Let's shake on it.' She put her hand in his. 'Happy reunion,' he said, and pulled her towards him. 'May I? For old times' sake?'

She coloured and offered him her cheek.

Lester frowned, pretending to be hurt. 'Fobbing me off with second-best already?'

Roland laughed. 'She's putting on the little sister act, Lester.'

'Is she? In that case I suppose I'll just have to play big brother and like it.' His lips touched her cheek.

'Has she changed, Lester?' Mr. Lennan wanted to know.

Lester's eyes moved over her face, seeing her well-marked eyebrows now drawn together in an embarrassed frown, her full lips, spoilt by a hint of discontent, her grey-blue eyes with a suggestion of unhappiness in their depths.

'Beyond recognition,' he said. 'If I had met her in the street, I would have passed her by.'

Elise pulled her hand from his. It was almost as if he had written her off as a nonentity. Although he had softened his words with a kindly smile, she knew by the tone of his voice that she had failed to pass his test. She had, in those few seconds, been tried and found wanting.

She forced herself to smile. 'You've changed, too.'

'Oh? In what way?'

'You've improved.'

He threw back his head and laughed with the others. 'That implies,' he said when they had stopped, 'that in the past there was room for improvement. Tell me, how have I improved? In looks? In manner?'

She considered him, her head on one side. 'Yes, in looks. You used to wear glasses.'

'Ah, I still do—contact lenses. That fooled you, didn't it?'

'In manner—well, I can't tell yet, can I? I remember that you often annoyed me. You were so high-handed. And you always laughed at me.'

'My word, you did think a lot of me in the old days! Now the truth's coming out.'

'What are you doing about lunch, Lester?' Mr. Lennan asked. 'Can we persuade you to share ours?'

Lester looked enquiringly at Elise.

'You're welcome to stay, Lester,' she said. 'It's only cold meat and salad, but——'

' "Only"? It's my favourite dish,' he joked. Elise turned to go. 'You're quite sure, Elise?' She saw his mocking smile and wondered what was coming. 'You don't still hate my guts and want to get rid of me?'

'I'll answer those two questions in a few weeks' time.' She stopped in the doorway. 'Or are you just passing through?'

'No. My grandfather sent an S.O.S. His firm's in such a mess administratively that he asked me to come and take over and pull him out of it. So I resigned my job and here I am.'

She frowned. 'So that means you've come to stay?'

'It does. Don't look so disappointed,' he laughed. 'We're old friends, after all.'

'You were Roland's friend,' she answered quietly. 'You were never mine.' Before she closed the door, she saw the smile in his eyes grow cold.

It was after lunch. The washing up was behind them and they were relaxing in the sitting-room in front of a roaring fire which Mr. Lennan had declared they needed, in spite of an efficient central heating system. 'It may be old-fashioned,' he would say, 'but it's a point of warmth to gather round.'

Warmth was something Harold Lennan seemed to need these days. Tall, carrying well the rotundity common to

11

some men of his age, his face, when caught off guard and without the good humour which was an important part of his personality, reflected the need for the hard shell of solitude into which he had withdrawn after the death of his wife.

Since that event five years before, he had assumed a veneer of unemotionalism which, his daughter guessed, covered an underlying and inconsolable sadness. His attitude of apparent acceptance of the inevitable, of whatever came along was, she suspected, a salve for the deep pain caused by the terrible blow life had dealt him—the loss of his beloved wife.

But perversely that loss seemed to have bound the family together more securely than her continued presence might have done. Sometimes Harold would look at his two children with amused despair. 'They won't leave me,' he would say. 'We're three single units fused into one. I'm destined never to be a grandfather.'

'Where are you living, Lester?' Roland asked.

'In digs at present, in a couple of rooms offered to me by an acquaintance of my grandfather's housekeeper. They'll do until I can move in with my grandfather. He's having a room prepared for me.'

'Has your granddad still got Mrs. Dennis?' Mr. Lennan asked. Lester nodded. 'So he's kept her all these years! They're two such awkward characters I'd have thought a clash would have been inevitable long before now.'

Lester laughed. 'From what I can gather, in the early days there were many clashes, but it seems that Mrs. Dennis now has him just where she wants him. He thinks he's the boss of the household, but she knows she is!' They laughed.

Lester looked at Elise curled up in an armchair, her feet lifted and tucked beneath her. Her head was resting on a cushion and she was staring into the yellow flames licking greedily up the chimney.

12

'Talking of boss, Elise,' he said, and waited until she turned her head towards him. Her eyes were distant and dreamy and he leaned forward and moved his hand from side to side in front of her face. 'Are you receiving me?'

She smiled. 'I heard every word you said.'

'That makes a change,' her brother commented. 'Sometimes it's almost impossible to communicate with that girl. She lives in a world of her own.'

'Talking of boss,' Lester repeated, looking at Roland, 'does she work for her living?'

'Of course I do!' She was fully aroused now and annoyed that he was talking about her as though she was too unintelligent to answer for herself. 'Part-time, in a hi-fi shop.'

He seemed puzzled. 'In a shop? But haven't you had any training?'

'Yes, in secretarial studies. I started off by working in the office at the back of the shop, then Mr. Pollard asked if I'd mind helping him serve the customers.'

'It's quite useful having her there,' Roland said. 'She gets things at a discount for us. You should see the expensive equipment she's got upstairs in her room.'

Lester smiled and his eyes were provocative. 'Perhaps she'll invite me up there to look at it some time.'

'It's no good, Lester. She's not that sort of a girl.'

Lester studied her for a long time. Embarrassed, she turned away from his scrutiny. 'No,' he said flatly, 'I can see she's not.'

Mr. Lennan stood and stretched, turning his back to the fire which was dying down now. 'It's not for want of offers, though, is it, Elise?'

'An offer,' his son corrected. 'Her boss, Phil Pollard, offers her his hand and his fortune (and I mean his fortune —he's got two or three thriving branches in other towns) at regular intervals.'

'Oh?' Lester contemplated her. 'And what's wrong with that?'

'A lot,' said Harold, pausing at the door. 'He's just past fifty, only a few years younger than I am.' He went out.

Lester laughed and taunted, 'Is that the best you can do, Elise?'

'She's ice-cold, Lester. She's got no interest in men.'

'Therefore men have no interest in her.' His eyes skated scathingly over her careless appearance and her unmade-up face. His expression, when he had finished, dismissed her as totally devoid of physical attraction, at least as far as he was concerned. She bunched up a cushion under her head and pressed her burning cheek against it.

He rose and walked to the french windows, staring out at the garden. 'So that's where your father is, Roland. What does he find to do out there in February?'

'Plenty. Gardening is his hobby. Even when it's in perfect order—to us—he's dissatisfied with it. If there's no work to do, he makes it!'

Lester grew reminiscent. 'In that case, it's a good job there are no kids around to play cricket on that lawn nowadays. Remember how we used to take it in turns to have the bat and bowl to one another?'

'We broke a few windows in our time, didn't we?' Roland looked round at his sister, who had not stirred from the armchair. 'And—nearly—a few heads. Remember that celebrated occasion when Elise got in the way?'

Lester winced. 'Good heavens, yes. I shrink from the thought.'

'I'd bowled to you, hadn't I?' Roland said, 'and you swung the bat up over your shoulder ready to take a swipe at the ball, Elise ran across in front of you and the bat made hard and heavy contact with her head.'

Lester put a hand to his own head as if it hurt to think of it. 'And she went flying across the lawn and lay there screaming. I thought I'd killed her, or at least cracked her

14

head open! But astonishingly, the doctor couldn't find anything seriously wrong.'

'She never forgave you for that incident. Did you know?'

Lester walked from the window and stood looking down at her. She stared up at him, the reflected firelight flickering in her eyes.

'Is that so, Elise? You never forgave me?'

She shook her head. 'And when after that you kept calling me "cricket ball" I absolutely hated you.'

Roland joined his friend. 'Then there was the day she had her own back. You put your hands round her head and pretended to "bowl" her to me.'

'Yes, I certainly remember. She turned on me and bit me, vicious little devil that she was. Her teeth went so deep I nearly had to have stitches in the wound.'

He watched for her reaction, but she made no response, just stared into the embers. Lester, hands in pockets, dipped his head in her direction. He asked, half jokingly, 'Is she always as quiet and subdued as this?'

Roland nodded. 'Nothing seems to arouse her these days.'

'Nothing?' asked Lester. 'Nothing at all, Elise?' His grin was provocative. 'Is that a challenge?'

She gazed steadfastly at him but did not move.

'My word,' he went on, 'she's changed even more than I thought she had. Where's the little spitfire she used to be? I can remember her screams whenever she didn't get her own way. She was a little horror, wasn't she, Roland?' He smiled as he watched the annoyance in her eyes increase. 'I can remember saying I didn't envy you having her as a sister, and that I wouldn't have her as my sister at any price.'

They laughed, enjoying the joke at her expense, and she was plunged straight back into the past. She was a child again and they were two maddening boys, superior in age, size and intellect, and she was a helpless, furious little girl, defenceless against their masculinity. And she wanted to

15

use her teeth to get her own back. She flushed heavily and bit her lip. Lester grinned and she could almost hear him thinking, 'At last, a positive reaction.'

Roland bent down to make up the fire and picked up the empty coal bucket. He said he wouldn't be long and went outside to fill it.

Lester threw himself into the other armchair and there was silence for a while. The fresh coal on the fire sparked and hissed and flames shot upwards, blue-green and yellow, as if overjoyed at having been brought back to life.

'So the vicious tiger cub turned tamely and disappointingly into a little mouse.' The taunt, spoken like the ending of a child's story, came from him goading, chafing like an irritant, prodding her out of her impassivity. But she merely moved her shoulders, shrugging them as if to throw off an aggravation.

He went on, his tone still provocative, 'So you never really forgave me for what I did to you?' She shook her head. 'Even though it was an accident.' He watched her closely. 'Now I'll show you something.' He sat forward. 'Come here, Elise.'

His commanding tone annoyed her, and for a moment she did not move. Then, feeling again like a child being dominated and ordered about by her brother's infuriating friend, she uncurled herself slowly from the armchair and walked across the rug to stand in front of him, pushing her hair back with both hands and smoothing the creases from her skirt.

He lifted his right hand and with his left forefinger indicated an area on the back of his right thumb. 'Look closely. It's a scar, isn't it? Your scar, the one your teeth left behind all those years ago. That was no accident. It was put there deliberately by a vindictive little fiend called Elise Lennan. I can never forget her, can I? Whether I want to or not, I'll have to explain it away to everyone who asks about it, my wife when I get one, my kids and my grandchildren. So

16

I've got it with me, that reminder of you, as long as I live.'
He pulled her down on to the arm of his chair. 'Now, if she
couldn't forgive me for something that was accidental, why
should I forgive her for something that was inflicted intentionally?'

She jerked away from him, trying to avoid having to
answer his question, but he held on to her wrist. She shook
her head helplessly. 'I'm sorry, Lester, I had no idea ...
But,' she looked at the scar again and frowned, 'there's
nothing I can do about it now, is there?'

'Nothing that would have any material value, no. Er—
just a thought,' a gleam came into his eyes, 'you could do
something that might help to heal the wound in other ways.'
He lowered his voice to a whisper, a maddening, gloating
whisper, 'You could kiss it better.'

She caught her breath and stared at him. 'You can't be
serious!'

He saw her doubt and lifted his hand towards her mouth.
'Go on. After all these years of carrying that unpleasant
reminder of you with me, I think I deserve something in the
nature of an apology, an act of obeisance, the administering
of a balm, by you who inflicted it on me in the first place.'

Overcome by a ridiculous sense of guilt, she moved as if
under hypnosis and her hand stretched out to take hold of
his, but as her fingers made contact with his flesh, she became aware of what was happening. He was her big
brother's infuriating friend all over again, laughing at her
and taunting her as he used to do in the past. And she had
almost fallen into his well-laid trap.

Horrified that she had even considered doing his bidding,
angry that she had almost permitted herself to be lowered
into a state of servility because of something that had
happened between them so many years before that she
could not now accept responsibility for it, she broke away
from him violently.

She stood for a moment staring down at him, incensed

17

beyond words at his subtle manipulation of the situation like a clever lawyer placing the guilt on the wrong person. Then she turned and ran from the room, shutting the door on his derisive laughter.

Elise relaxed on Sundays. She cooked the lunch and tidied up, and spent the rest of the day doing very little at all. Her part-time job at Phil Pollard's shop left her afternoons free. That was when she cleaned the house and washed the family's clothes.

Her father had often told her she need not go to work. With two substantial salaries coming in, he would say—his and Roland's—he was quite willing to give her all the money she wanted for her own personal needs.

But Elise had stubbornly refused to accept the role of full-time housekeeper. She did not want to be financially dependent on her father and in any case could not regard the work she did in the house as a 'job', with her father as employer. She did it, she often told him, because she was his daughter and happened to be fond of him!

The two men helped her whenever they could. Sometimes, during the college vacations, her father would potter about in the kitchen experimenting with savoury dishes which he saw in Elise's cookery books and which, he said, looked too mouth-watering to resist.

Lunch was over and she was on her way upstairs when the doorbell rang. Surprised at having a caller on a Sunday afternoon, she opened the door.

'Hallo, Lester,' she said in flat tones to the man on the doorstep, and moved back to let him in. She could not understand why her pulse rate should have accelerated so alarmingly just because Lester Kings had come to the house.

'Hallo, Elise, Roland in?'

She nodded. 'Upstairs in his room. Would you like to go up?'

Her voice sounded even and controlled and she deliberately eliminated any trace of warmth from her expression as she looked at him. His smile died away at the sight of her lifeless face.

He frowned and asked sharply, 'Which room? The same as he used to have?'

She nodded again and he sprinted up the stairs. She followed and went into her own bedroom. She heard her brother's welcome and for the next half-hour listened to their raised voices and their rollicking laughter with an envy so powerful it frightened her.

She had never felt the need for company before. Her nature was solitary—a trait she had inherited from her father. It was a fact she never quarrelled with and had never tried to alter. She had always felt different from other girls of her own age. She hadn't needed friends as they had done. There was an obstacle within her which had prevented the spontaneous interchange of thoughts and words and laughter which seemed to be an essential part of other girls' lives.

Her brother had always been there to give her companionship if she felt she needed any. Now it seemed that, almost imperceptibly, and within only a few hours of Lester Kings' return into their lives, things had already started to change. And the thought filled her with fear—and foreboding.

She sighed, telling herself not to be foolish. She had intended listening to some records but the mood had passed. Instead, she stared out of the window, watching her father at work in the back garden, seeing the bare branches of the apple trees, still enslaved by the paralytic hand of winter, moving stiffly in the wind. She knew there must be the beginnings of buds on those branches, but they were out of her range of vision.

Her thoughts turned inwards as she sought for solace inside herself, but her emotions were like rigid leafless

19

branches, stripped bare of foliage, stunted by the iron control she exercised over them every day of her life. She was as dead inside as winter and if any buds existed giving promise of flowers to come then she could not see them.

Roland's door opened. He called, 'Elise, are you in there?' He knocked and walked in, with Lester close behind.

Her bleak expression was familiar to her brother and he did not seem to notice it. Lester's eyes flicked over her face and took in the desolate droop of her shoulders.

'We're going for a walk,' Roland said. 'Coming?'

'Where to?'

'Your favourite retreat, Dawes Hall woods.'

'All right, I'll get ready.'

'I thought you'd say that. I told you, Lester, didn't I? She haunts the place.'

'So you said.'

Roland went out and Elise picked up a comb from the dressing-table and ran it through her hair. Lester lounged against the wall and watched. She wished he would go. She dusted some powder over her cheeks and turned quickly from her own reflection.

Lester went on leaning against the wall, hands in pockets, watching her, saying nothing. She wished he would talk, would even make a joke at her expense, anything but stand there with that merciless, dissecting look on his face as though he were analysing every particle of her body.

Her jacket was in the wardrobe and she reached inside to get it, wishing she could hide in there until he had gone. She felt as if the antennae of his mind were reaching down into her very depths.

She swung round to face him asking sharply, 'Is there something wrong with me?'

He eased himself upright and smiled slightly. 'Since you've asked me and since I'm an old friend of the family,

20

I'll answer the question frankly—yes, there's quite a lot wrong with you. But that isn't why I was looking at you. I was just trying to find out what makes you tick.'

'And what's the answer?'

'I don't know. You remain an enigma—for the moment.' He stood back to let her precede him down the stairs. Roland was waiting in the hall.

'I've told Dad we're going out.' He held the door open for her and Lester, then shut it behind him.

They walked along the pavement away from the main road and crossed a bridge which spanned the railway line. Soon they were climbing a hill towards the fields and Lester walked with a certainty which revealed that he, like his companions, knew every inch of the way.

They made for an avenue of elm trees and walked along it three abreast, with Roland in the middle. The broad tree-lined drive was bordered on each side by fields and it bore left to pass a country mansion, now in ruins.

But they went straight on making for the woods which were an attractive part of the Dawes Hall estate. The former owner had died and the people of the neighbourhood were hoping that the present owners would sell the place to someone who would restore the house—and the fields and woods attached to the property—to their former glory.

The public had constant and unimpeded access to the estate, not by order of the present owners, but by custom and neglect. There was not a single fence left intact.

'I remember when we used to come here as kids,' Lester said, turning to look back at the old mansion standing gaunt and decaying, its windows smashed, its doors swinging loose in the breeze. 'The place was magnificent then. Now look at it.'

'The old man died,' Roland told him. 'His relatives have been fighting over the property for years.'

'I know. My grandfather told me.'

The woods were long and narrow and were bordered by

21

fields. Winding its way through the trees was a well-worn path, hard and rutted in a summer drought, in winter rains an impossible bog.

'There's the tree we used to climb.' Lester walked to the base of a hornbeam and patted its trunk. 'The footholds are still there. What about it, Elise?' he joked. 'You first?'

She laughed and his eyes lingered momentarily on her face.

'I remember the day she got struck up there,' Roland remarked. 'I tried to get her down and she screamed and said she didn't want me, she wanted you.'

'Yes, I remember,' Lester said thoughtfully, his eyes still on her. 'I did get her down, too, partly by persuasion and partly by brute force. After that she insisted on holding my hand all the way home. Do you remember, Elise?'

She coloured slightly and nodded.

'That must have been before the rot set in, before she began to hate me in earnest.' He gave her a challenging smile, but she did not respond.

They moved on and Elise said, 'I remember going for walks with the two of you and listening to what you were saying and trying to understand, but it was way above my head, intellectually as well as physically!'

'And no wonder,' Roland said. 'If I can think back that far, we spent most of our time discussing things like politics and philosophy, didn't we, Lester?'

He nodded. 'We thought we knew all the answers to all the questions in those days. And I remember her,' he indicated Elise, looking up at us and asking "what's this?" and "what's that?" Of course we never condescended to answer. I remember something else, too. She insisted on walking between us and holding our hands like this,' he caught her hand and held it, 'and asking us to swing her.' He grinned at Roland. 'Shall we, for old times' sake?'

'No, thanks, Lester,' Roland laughed. 'I've outgrown it, even if she hasn't!'

Elise took her hand from Lester's and pushed it into her jacket pocket. He tutted softly and said, 'I thought you were going to hold it all the way home, just like you used to do.'

She laughed again and he glanced down at her, smiling. She smiled back, feeling the blood racing through her veins and her emotions stirring from their long, long sleep. She was sure the birdsong seemed louder and the sun brighter in the clear sky.

'Are your parents still living in Newcastle, Lester?' Roland asked, talking across Elise who was still in the centre.

'Yes. And after I qualified, I was lucky enough to get a job near home, so I lived with them.'

'And Nina's their next-door neighbour? That's convenient, isn't it?' They exchanged smiles.

'Very,' said Lester.

Elise looked up sharply. A thrust of fear pierced her armour like a bullet. 'Who's Nina?' she asked, dreading the answer.

'My fiancée,' Lester said.

CHAPTER II

WHEN they arrived home from their walk, Elise made tea for them all. Her father came in from the garden and they drank it in the firelight. Elise curled up in her favourite armchair while the men talked. She did not attempt to join in. Instead she watched the flames licking and darting greedily round the logs her brother had thrown on the fire.

Her face reflected the melancholy of her thoughts. She could not understand why the sun, which had seemed to be rising on her world, had set again so finally and irreversibly. She felt she had lost something she never even knew she

23

had and the feeling tormented her.

The men were discussing Alfred Kings, Lester's grand-father.

'So he's called you in to pull him out of the mess?' Harold was saying. 'I don't know whether you know it, but he's got a name in these parts for being an old rascal.'

'You've got a lot to live down, Lester,' Roland commented, holding out his cup for more tea.

Elise unwound herself from her comfortable position and refilled his cup, then her father's. She looked at Lester, pointing to the teapot and raising her eyebrows in query. He nodded and she filled his cup, too. She handed it back and he smiled at her, murmuring his thanks. She felt a warmth flooding through her which she knew was not caused by those flames roaring up the chimney, and which were methodically destroying the logs now charred almost beyond recognition.

'I've chatted to a few people already,' Lester said, 'and I've got some idea of local opinion. But my methods are radically different from my grandfather's and I certainly don't intend to follow in his footsteps.'

'One thing he can't seem to do,' Harold said, 'is keep his best workers. In my job—you know I teach surveying at the technical college?—I hear these things on the grapevine via the building students, and the best ones say they wouldn't work for "old Kings", as they call him, for a fortune.'

Lester shook his head, staring at the fire. 'I didn't know that. But I do know that his relations with his employees are bad. It seems he was constantly overruling his site manager and ordering stuff when it was not needed or at the wrong time, so they were getting deliveries of materials—tiles, cement and so on—long before they were necessary. Nor had he kept the accounts properly because he was trying to do it all himself.'

Elise gathered the cups and saucers on to the tray and carried them to the kitchen. She washed them and left them to drain. She could hear the men's voices and knew they were too absorbed in their discussion to miss her.

She went up to her bedroom and shut herself in. She sat on the bed and looked round the room which had been hers since childhood. There were books on the shelf her father had put up. The table, once piled high with children's comics, schoolgirl magazines and dolls' clothes now boasted proudly among the magazines and leaflets, a transistor radio, a portable television set and expensive hi-fi equipment.

She leaned on the windowsill and stared out at the garden. Down there on the lawn she could remember the scars—the grooves and ridges they had inflicted on it as children. She recalled how they used to scrape the lawn with the soles of their shoes and dig into it with their heels as they moved to and fro on the garden swing they used to have.

She could remember Lester tormenting her on it, pushing her on it so high she had been forced to scream to make him stop. Sometimes he had scrambled up and swung from the top bar, kicking out with his legs and threatening to drop down and land on her head if she didn't get off the seat.

More than anything else about him she remembered his taunts and his teasing and even now the feeling of resentment and hatred welled up in her as she remembered the Lester of long ago. Time had not thrown out the memory, it clung to her still.

She turned away from the window and sighed. This room was her world, the centre of her existence, the pivot round which her life revolved. There she could be herself, relaxed and at peace. It was her sanctuary, her hiding place and as such, she would share it with no one.

She changed into black trousers and an old black ribbed sweater which seemed to have tightened with each washing. But it did not matter what she looked like. She would not go downstairs until teatime and by then Lester would have gone.

She combed her hair until it fluffed out round her cheeks and slipped on a wide blue band to keep it tidy. She could not understand why, but there seemed to be an unmistakable improvement in her looks. She shrugged and turned away from the mirror.

She selected a record from the rack, placed it carefully on the turntable and extracted her elaborate and expensive headphones from the pile of leaflets under which they were buried. She lowered the headphones carefully over her head, kicked off her shoes and stretched out on the bed, raising her hands to support her head. She closed her eyes and escaped into the magic world of stereophonic sound.

She lay there for some time, cocooned in the music, wrapped in a blanket of pleasurable tones and harmonies.

Something alerted her, some warning bell in her brain started ringing. Someone was in the room. She held her breath and opened her eyes. Lester was standing beside the bed, hands in pockets, legs slightly apart, looking down at her. There was no smile on his face, not even the teasing glint in his eyes to which she had become conditioned since childhood. He was looking at her instead with a pity, a depth of compassion which dismayed and frightened her. She would rather have had his taunts and his mockery than his pity.

She sat up, swinging her feet to the floor. She lifted off the headphones and leaned across to stop the record player. Lester lowered himself on to the bed beside her. He was smiling now.

'I did knock, but when you didn't answer I took an old friend's licence and walked in.' He looked at the head-phones now lying on her lap. 'So you've achieved your ultimate goal—you have totally and uncompromisingly shut out the world.' He shook his head. 'You know, you are the most extraordinary female I've ever come across.'

She swung her hair loosely round the back of her neck with a nervous gesture.

'Just a little mouse, aren't you? Tucked away in your hidey-hole, looking on at life, standing aside, not taking part. Where's all that liveliness, that fighting back I used to see in my old friend Roland's infuriating little sister?'

Her eyes clouded. 'Gone. I've faced life now, been disillusioned, learnt the truth about living.'

'Good grief! You sound as if you've received the jilting of a lifetime at the hands of some notorious playboy!' He leaned away from her and his eyes moved into shadow. 'Have you?'

'No, nothing like that. At least I'd have lived a little if that had happened.'

He grinned. 'Such bitterness, and she's only twenty-six!' He changed his tone. 'Good heavens, girl, you haven't even started living. It's yourself you're disillusioned with, not life. You're locked in a castle of your own making, untouched, unattainable, beyond the reach of any man.' He looked her over assessingly, lazily. 'You should always wear clothes like that.'

She coloured and looked down. 'Now I suppose you're going to advise me to use cosmetics to hide my blemishes.'

'The only cosmetics you need are happiness and a good relationship with a member of the opposite sex. They would transform you, improve you beyond words.'

'Thank you very much,' she said sourly.

He laughed. 'Just giving you advice as an old friend.' He went on, 'But I'm serious, Elise. The right man would cure all your troubles.'

She frowned. 'When the right man—as you put it—comes along, I won't even recognise him, and even if I did, he wouldn't want me.'

'Oh, snap out of it, girl. Your self-abasement makes me sick!'

She retorted sulkily, 'I'm sorry if you don't like my conversation, but I didn't invite you in here.'

He opened his mouth to retaliate, saw the desolation in her eyes and said gently, 'We're fighting again, aren't we—just like old friends.' She gave him a grudging smile and after a pause he said, 'I was sorry to hear about your mother. You must miss her.' She nodded, unaware of the 'lost' look that had crept into her eyes.

'You have a lot of responsibilities on your shoulders, looking after the house and your father and brother.'

She shrugged. 'Some women of my age have a husband and two or three kids. I can't grumble.' She looked up at him and saw the pity again.

What could she do to convince this man that she didn't need his pity, that she was supremely content with her life as she lived it?

'Your fiancée, Nina—what's she like, Lester?'

He seemed momentarily disconcerted by her question. 'Oh,' he said, 'she's fair-haired, pretty, not very tall. She's training to be a nurse at a large hospital in Newcastle.'

'When are you getting married?'

'Not for a while yet. She wants to qualify first.'

Elise looked up at him, startled. 'Did you say she's *training* to be a nurse?' He nodded. 'Then she's not very old?'

He looked uncomfortable and stared at the carpet. 'No. She's eighteen.'

'*Eighteen?* But Lester, you're—thirty-four!'

'Well?' His eyes were belligerent.

'That makes her sixteen years younger than you are.'

He turned on her. 'So what if she is? Do you think I can't add up? That I'm not already aware of the fact?'

She shrank from his anger. 'I'm sorry. I was surprised, that's all.'

He lifted his shoulders. 'All right, I'm sorry for jumping on you. It's just that—it worries me sometimes being so much older.'

Elise could find nothing to say. It was so plainly a prob-

28

lem to which he was struggling to find an answer, a situation which he was constantly and unsuccessfully trying to rationalise that it was useless to offer him a balm in the form of platitudes.

He got up and wandered restlessly round the room. He bent down and picked up something half-hidden under the cushion on a chair. He held it out. 'This doll—haven't I seen it before?'

'You should have done—you gave it to me!'

'I remember now—I gave it as a peace offering for bashing you on the head. It cost me six or seven weeks' pocket money.' He tugged at the dress. 'It's lost an arm.'

She pulled at the expanding strap of her wrist-watch. 'Yes. I—I was so angry with you, I tore it off the first day I had it.'

She looked up full of apology and saw his shock and disbelief. He said, 'You really did hate me, didn't you!'

He dropped the doll on the chair as if he could not bear to touch it and stared at the books on the shelf. Then he moved to the table.

'What's this intriguing piece of equipment?'

She slipped on her shoes and joined him. 'That's a cassette recorder cum radio and record player, all in one and all stereo. It's called a "music centre".'

He pointed to two rectangular boxes. 'And I suppose those are the two loudspeakers.'

'Yes.' Her eyes were bright. 'Don't you think it's fabulous?'

He smiled and remained determinedly sceptical. 'I don't know till I hear it, do I?' He fingered the controls. 'And is this your means of escape, your magic carpet that wafts you away from reality into your dream-world?'

She ignored the mockery behind his words. 'Look,' she pointed out, 'here's the tuning dial, these selector buttons are for tuning, volume and so on, and those are coloured lights that show which button is pressed in.'

She demonstrated and he said, 'Oh, very pretty.'

'This is the microphone input, that's the recording level meter, that's the headphone socket——'

'What are you trying to do, sell me the thing?'

She laughed. 'It cost an awful lot of money.'

'That's no way to tempt a potential customer. You'd better withdraw that remark quickly if you want to make a sale!'

'I don't. It took me months to save up for it and I certainly don't want to part with it now.'

He was looking at her and she caught an odd expression in his eyes. She turned away, embarrassed, unaware that her enthusiasm had brought an attractive flush to her cheeks and an unaccustomed brightness to her eyes.

'Go on,' he urged, 'tell me more.' He picked up the headphones. 'Why do you use these when you could listen to two perfectly good speakers?'

'Well, partly because Dad does a lot of work at home and he can't stand the noise——'

Lester nodded. 'I can sympathise with him.'

'And partly——' She stopped. How much could she tell him without giving away too much of herself?

He seemed to sense her struggle and waited patiently for her to continue. She said, hoping he would not laugh at her as he used to do when they were younger, 'Partly because it's such a wonderful experience to listen on headphones.' She stopped again.

'Go on,' he said, 'tell me why.'

Encouraged by his apparent interest, she did go on. She spoke with difficulty, like someone who had been in solitary confinement for months and found it difficult to communicate with another human being. 'It—it involves the entire body. You close your eyes and—shut out the whole world. It's a sensation of pure delight.' She stole a look at him and saw the absolute seriousness of his expression. He was not laughing at her, so she took courage and went on, 'It's so personal, you feel it's your music and it becomes part of you. You feel a reciprocity between you and the music and you're in complete and utter sympathy with it.' She stopped again.

'I'm with you, go on.' He spoke so softly she was hardly aware that he had spoken at all.

'You want to listen to it alone. Solitude is essential, because anyone else in the room takes away the pleasure. You're so afraid they're going to interrupt.'

He nodded as if he understood.

She laughed, embarrassed again. 'I think it must have some effect on your nervous system, because you actually feel tingles down your spine.'

'So it's a bit like a drug,' he mused, 'you feel drunk or soothed according to what you're listening to. And when it's over and you emerge from it, it's like coming out of a dream.'

She nodded and was surprised at the extent of his understanding.

His tone altered slightly. 'It's also the height of selfishness. It's self-indulgence brought to a fine art. The rest of the world can go to hell because you're all that matters.' His eyes grew critical. 'You're a hedonist to the core, aren't you?'

She frowned, uncertain now. He was holding a mirror up to her and she did not like what she saw. She offered him the headphones.

'Why don't you listen, then you'll know what I'm talking about.'

He did not take them. 'I'm not the solitary you seem to be. I'm a sociable creature. I love my fellow men.' He grinned. 'And women.'

He had lightened the atmosphere considerably and, she guessed, deliberately. He eyed the headphones. 'All the same, I think I might sample them.'

He sat on the bed and took the headphones from her.

'Come on, show me how to put these things on.'

She helped him lower the headphones over his head until the earpieces covered his ears, but he held them away and asked, 'What am I going to listen to?'

'*Schéhérezade* by Rimsky-Korsakov. You must know it?'

'Yes, very well. So you're going to stir me to my emotional depths and arouse my passions, are you?' He gave a provocative grin. 'All right, go ahead. Set the record player going. But don't be surprised if you can't keep me under control when I've finished listening!'

Her heart jerked oddly at the look he gave her and she moved away, trying to put herself out of range of the magnetism which emanated from his body and which disturbed and worried her.

He stretched out on the bed and raised his hands to support his head as she had done. He closed his eyes and, like her, seemed lost to the world. She sat at the foot of the bed and although she could not hear the music herself—it was being channelled straight into the stereo headphones—she tried to follow it in her mind.

Now and then she stole a look at him, attempting to gauge his reactions. But his expression told her nothing. It was wholly serious and completely relaxed and as she studied his features, his well-shaped mouth with its sardonic twist even in repose, his heavily marked brows and the hint of arrogance about his whole facial structure, she was conscious of a response inside her which brought her close to panic.

He opened his eyes and smiled. Then he sighed and removed the headphones, handing them back to her but remaining where he was. 'Thanks, I've heard enough.'

She stopped the record player.

'Like the Sultan in the story, I've been tamed, but I'm in an emotional turmoil.' He made a dive for her hand and caught it, pulling her nearer. 'It was the passion in the love music that did it, the story of the prince and princess who

32

sing of their love for each other. It's a beautiful sequence, don't you agree?' She nodded. 'When you listen to this stuff,' he went on, 'doesn't it move you to want to make love, to indulge your passions? Or do you use it simply as a means of sublimating your desires?' He sat up and swung his feet to the floor, smiling mockingly. 'Or perhaps you don't have any desires?'

She jerked her hand away and he laughed. 'What's the matter? Don't you like it when I try to batter my way through your defences? I must say, they're pretty formidable. They're so impregnable they'd put any man off, believe me.'

So he was dismissing her yet again as an unattractive, undesirable nonentity. Although she admitted to herself that it was probably true, his dismissal nonetheless hurt her deeply.

His hand indicated the stereo equipment. 'Where did you get it?'

'Through the shop. Mr. Pollard let me have it at a discount.'

'Since he's got a hi-fi business, I take it he's an enthusiast, too?'

She nodded. 'He's got some marvellous equipment at his home.'

'Well, he's got a soft spot for you, hasn't he? So why don't you marry him? Think of the joy you'd get from his equipment!'

'You mean marry him for his stereo?' They laughed together. 'It would be a novel variation on the old theme of marrying a man for his money!'

They laughed again and she was aware of a feeling, quite alien to her, of sharing. Suddenly she felt frighteningly vulnerable. He seemed to have penetrated her barriers without even trying, like taking down the shutters from a boarded-up house and letting the sunshine come flooding in.

33

There was a stirring inside her like someone rousing from a state of prolonged unconsciousness. Lester Kings was no longer the childhood friend, the logical-thinking, neutral, dispassionate youth whom she had looked upon as another brother. He was a man, a stranger, an intruder into her private world, plundering her solitude and making off with her self-sufficiency.

She panicked. Somehow she had to shut him out again. She seized a record from the rack, put it on the turntable and set it going. She adjusted the headphones over her ears, lay back on the bed again and drifted away into the music. Before she closed her eyes, she saw him pick up a radio catalogue and flick through it.

She hoped he would take the hint and go, but he stayed on. After a while she opened her eyes and saw with a profound shock that he was watching her. Her heartbeats responded to the groundswell of excitement which surged through her body. She could not understand his expression.

She started up, her eyes wide and questioning. She lifted the headphones away from her ears as though trying to listen to something he had said, but he had not spoken a word. The magazine he had been looking at fell to the floor. He picked it up, replaced it on the table and went out.

She sat up, no longer able to commune with the music, no longer wanting to. He had gone and she wanted him back.

She felt a shaft of fear as if her security was being threatened, as if the very foundations on which her life was built were moving under her feet, like ground cracking open in an earthquake. He had turned her solitude into loneliness and it bore down on her, threatening to engulf her and making her afraid.

CHAPTER III

THE record department which Phil Pollard had had in mind for years at last became a reality. Listening booths, complete with headphones, had been installed and next morning the first delivery of records arrived. Elise helped her employer to unpack them and stack them side by side on the purpose-built shelves.

Phil told her as they worked, 'A young woman is coming to see me this morning. If I like her I'll put her in charge of the record section. My next-door neighbour knows her. Apparently she's been working in London, but wants a job nearer home. By the way,' his voice became confidential, 'her name's Mrs. Hill, but she's a widow—lost her husband soon after they were married. Car accident.' He shook his head sadly.

Elise visualised a slightly intolerant middle-aged woman, but Clare Hill, when she arrived, was far from middle-aged. She was young—just under thirty, Elise guessed—and attractive and lively. Phil took to her at once and offered her the job.

When Clare walked out of the office after the interview, Elise asked her 'When are you starting?' expecting the answer to be 'next week', but Clare said,

'Now, this minute. As I told Mr. Pollard, I'm eager, willing and ready for work!'

Clare Hill's personality, Elise discovered, was the kind that reached out to encompass everyone and even Elise, though normally reticent and shy in the presence of strangers, found herself responding with a warmth that equalled Clare's. She lost her reserve and talked more openly to her than she had ever talked to anyone before.

As Elise was leaving at lunch-time, Phil called her back. 'Did you know old man Kings' grandson is back in the district? Rumour has it he's going to run the old boy's business.'

Yes, Elise told him, she did know. 'He came to see us at the weekend.'

Phil looked at her sharply and Elise laughed, guessing that he had already married her off to him. 'He came to see my brother, not me. Anyway, he's engaged.'

Phil smiled with obvious relief but frowned again as he asked, 'Have you also heard the rumour that old Kings has bought Dawes Hall estate?' Now it was Elise who frowned. No, she hadn't heard, she said.

'And if Alfred Kings gets his hands on anything,' Phil went on, 'especially where there's land involved, it can only mean one thing—he intends to build there.'

Elise's throat tightened and her hand went to it. 'But surely he can't do that unless he gets planning permission, and the local authority wouldn't grant that, would they?'

Phil shook his head. 'That's the trouble—they've got planning permission already. Apparently Kings told the owners he'd only buy on that condition, so permission to build was applied for and they were successful. It put up the total price, of course, but old Kings didn't blink an eyelid, he's so wealthy.' Phil drew in his lips. 'I wish I knew how to stop the old devil.'

'But,' Elise said, still unwilling to accept it as an accomplished fact, 'we went for a walk in the woods on Sunday and Lester came with us. If they intended building on it, surely he would have said so?'

'Not necessarily. He wouldn't tell you his business, would he?'

No, Elise thought, not me. But he might have told my brother. She tackled Roland as soon as he arrived home that evening. To her horror, he admitted it.

'It's true, Elise, but Lester told me not to tell you. He probably didn't want to upset you.'

She exclaimed sarcastically, 'You're not trying to tell me that Lester Kings has suddenly turned considerate? It's much more likely that knowing how I feel about those woods, he didn't want any trouble.'

'Well,' her brother eyed her uncomfortably, 'he's coming this evening, so I'd better warn him in advance to be ready the onslaught, hadn't I?'

'He's coming here again?' she asked, dismayed. 'Why?'

'To phone his girl-friend. He says it's difficult doing it from his digs as the telephone's in the hall and he's sure his landlady listens to every word he says. Anyway,' he challenged, the big brother in him coming out, 'why shouldn't he come here? He's my friend. He can come any time he wants. He comes to see me, not you.' And with that crushing retort, he left her.

But whether Lester had come to see her or not, she was determined to see him. She was ready for him as soon as he stepped in the door. She confronted him like a demonstrator trying to get the better of a particularly stubborn and brawny policeman. And, she discovered to her cost, with about as much success.

'Roland tells me,' she assailed him, 'that you and your grandfather are intending to build on the Dawes Hall estate, including the woods.'

His eyes narrowed. 'Well, what of it?'

'It's outrageous! How can you even think of tearing down those trees and destroying all that beauty, just to put more money into your pockets? Can't you build on the fields around the Hall and leave the woods intact?'

He said quietly, 'It's not practicable to leave the woods intact. They're an integral part of the estate. If we left them, they would cut right across the area we're going to develop. Anyway, with land values as high as they are at present, we couldn't possibly afford to leave them as they are.'

She tackled him from another more personal angle. 'When we went for a walk on Sunday why did you tell Roland, but not me? Were you afraid?'

He laughed incredulously. 'Afraid of *you*? I didn't tell you, my dear Elise, because I knew Roland had enough sense to see the matter in a reasonable light. But I knew damned well you'd make a fuss. And I was right, wasn't I? Witness your performance now.'

Her voice rose sharply in a desperate attempt to make him see reason. 'You'll have all the local people against you. You don't suppose they'll sit back and watch those woods being destroyed without doing something to stop you, do you?'

'They can't stop us. Planning permission has been granted. My grandfather and I own the whole estate. It's ours to develop as we like.'

'They'll—they'll go to law, take out an injunction to stop you.'

'Oh, will they? It's not as simple as you think. And anyway, I have my methods for dealing with people like that. And with people like you, who put aesthetics before bread and butter needs, so be warned.'

'You're nothing better than a vandal,' she cried, sensing defeat and falling back on abuse. 'You're ruthless, you're barbaric, you delight in destruction!'

He exchanged a condescending smile with Roland. 'Now she's reverting to childhood. She knows she's lost, so she's salving her pride by calling me names.' He shrugged and turned back to her. 'If it gives you pleasure, go ahead, insult me. It doesn't worry me.' He saw the violence in her eyes and the tightly clenched fists and smiled derisively. 'You'll be plunging right back into the past in a minute and start hitting out at me as you used to do when I annoyed you as a child.'

She paled at his mockery. 'If I do, it won't be my fault. It'll be yours. You're driving me to it. You're so—so sure of yourself, so—so supercilious, so darned arrogant. You're quite convinced you're right, aren't you?'

Roland intervened, knowing his sister's unpredictable

38

temper and afraid of the consequences if his friend pro-voked her too far. 'Next to music, Lester, those woods are her greatest solace.'

But Roland's intervention seemed only to have made matters worse.

'Solace?' Lester asked scathingly. 'What does she need solace for at her age? Go out and live, girl. Get yourself a man—if you can. Do something to bring yourself to life.' He studied her with contempt. 'You know, if anyone had told me seventeen years ago that you'd grow up like this, like a dull, lifeless ice-cold doll—although that word has sensual connotations which couldn't possibly be applied to you—I'd have laughed in their faces.'

His calculated insults stirred her to an anger she had never felt before against another human being and she knew that if he did not stop provoking her, she would be unable to control it.

'Thanks for those few well-chosen compliments, Lester Kings,' she choked, 'spoken as offensively as only you know how. It's obvious *you* haven't changed, even if I have. No wonder I hated your guts all those years ago. I've never really forgiven you for the way you used to treat me when I was a child.' She grew conscious of a pain in the palms of her hands from the pressure of her finger nails. 'If it's possible, I hate you even more now than I did then.' To her annoyance her voice became unsteady. 'Why did you have to come back? Why didn't you stay where you were, hundreds of miles away? Why can't you go back again?'

He pushed his hands into his pockets and smiled at Roland. 'She says she hates me.' His eyes swung back to her. 'All right, Elise, so you hate me. Go and pull another arm off that doll I gave you. It won't hurt me, and I'm sure it will give you the greatest satisfaction!'

She was thrust into the past again and cried out in anguish at her helplessness in the face of his indifference and self-possession. She felt the fury inside her boiling over and made a wild movement with her hands towards him. He remained cool and unmoved and stood his ground.

Roland flung out his arm to restrain her and she turned and ran wildly up the stairs. As she reached the landing, she heard Lester say, with affected surprise,

'Good God, I've brought her to life!'

She flung herself on the bed in the darkness, seized her pillow, pummelled it, then, sobbing, buried her face in it.

By the time she had calmed down, it was late. She reached out and switched on the table lamp. Her father would be expecting his usual cup of tea. She went into the bathroom and splashed her face with cold water. In the bedroom she dusted her face with powder and peered at herself. It was no good, she could do nothing to disguise the desolation in her eyes.

She combed her hair dispiritedly and turned from the dreary image which scowled back at her in the mirror. As she went down the stairs, Lester was in the hall. He was talking on the phone to his fiancée.

'That's all very well, darling,' he was saying, 'but you could have written a few lines. A postcard would have been better than nothing. What? Yes, all right, I'll forgive you. But don't let it happen again.'

Elise reached the foot of the stairs when he spoke again.

'No, not from my digs, from a friend's house, Roland Lennan's. I told you about him. He's a very old friend of mine. Yes, he's about my age.' Elise was creeping past when his hand shot out and grasped her wrist. 'No, darling, he doesn't live alone, he lives with his father and sister.' Elise tried to pull her wrist away, but Lester held on. 'What's his sister like?' He grinned. 'No, she's not older than her brother, she's younger, so that means she's younger than I am—eight years, in fact.'

Elise tried to free herself again, but was forced by his hold to stand beside him. 'What's she like? Er—let me see,

40

she's standing next to me. In fact, she won't let me alone.' His provocative grin drove Elise to make a desperate attempt to free herself, but his hand tightened. 'She's—er —fairly tall. No, shorter than I am. Her hair, let me see—it's a light brown. What? Mousey? Yes, that would be a very good description—of the girl as well as her hair.' He dealt quite easily with the sudden jerk away from him. 'She's got blazing eyes,' his gaze moved down, 'a bosom heaving with passion——'

'Lester,' she hissed, 'let—me—go!'

He ignored her plea. 'Good legs, and a shape that—well, I'll leave that to your imagination. In fact, all in all, she's stunning. Yes, I'm trying to make you jealous. Is she after me?' He raised his eyes and smiled gloatingly. 'I'll say she's after me. In fact I know for certain that as soon as I come off this phone, she's going to throw herself at me.'

Elise lifted up her wrist and his hand came with it. She carried it towards her mouth and opened her teeth to sink them into his flesh. He realised with a shock what she was going to do and sank his nails viciously into her instead. Then with an angry gesture he let her go. He waved her away and turned his back on her.

Provoked beyond words, she went into the kitchen, nursing her bruised wrist. She was making the tea when Lester appeared at the door. He leaned against it and watched her.

'You nearly did it again, didn't you?' he said. 'You nearly bit me—the other hand this time. You haven't lost your nasty habits over the years.'

'What did you expect me to do—put it to my lips and kiss it?'

'You might have got an unexpected response if you had. More pleasant, I can assure you,' he drawled, 'than the one you actually got. Behave like other girls—try it some time, and see what happens.'

She put milk into the cups and poured the tea. 'Even if I

41

did, it wouldn't be your hand I'd choose. After the way you were insulting me to your fiancée——'

'Insulting you? You should have been flattered. The way I was promoting your image would have done credit to the country's top publicity man.'

'They were all lies, nothing but lies.' She turned away. 'You were only saying those things to make her jealous. I suppose you're afraid that with her up there in Newcastle and you down here in the south, it's a case of "out of sight, out of mind".'

He straightened himself slowly and walked across to stand behind her. He put his hands on her waist. 'Take some advice from an old friend, Elise. One, keep your nose out of what is definitely not your business. Two, don't let your inadequacy and ineffectiveness with the opposite sex turn you sour. And three,' he turned her round, 'take a long hard look at yourself. Believe me, from a man's point of view, you've got what it takes. It's just your mental attitude that's all wrong. Do something about that, and you could have any man you want.'

She twisted away because she could not bear the touch of his hands. 'If I wanted a man—which I don't—I could have one, just like that.' She snapped her fingers.

'Ah yes, your boss. Let me see, he's—how many years older than you—twenty-five? You'd have to be pretty hard up to——'

'*Will you leave me alone?*'

He shrugged and went into the sitting-room to join Roland and his father. Elise composed herself with difficulty and followed him with the tray.

'So it's true, Lester,' Mr. Lennan was saying, 'that rumour about chopping down Dawes Hall woods.'

Roland glanced apprehensively at his sister as she handed him his cup of tea, but Lester did not even raise his eyes. He merely took the cup she offered him and said,

'Yes, it's true. It's a pity, I agree, but——'

'Don't tell my daughter. She'll never let you live it down.'

'Elise will have to learn to accept the idea, like the rest of the community.' He flicked a glance at her stony face. 'It's the price of progress.'

'Does Phil Pollard know?' Roland asked Elise.

'Yes. He told me he'd heard the rumour too.' Her hostile stare challenged Lester. 'He said if it was true he was going to think of a way of stopping you.'

'Let him try. He won't succeed.'

'What makes you so sure? When Phil Pollard makes up his mind to do something, he usually succeeds.'

Lester looked amused. 'Really? In that case, there's hope for him yet where you're concerned, isn't there?'

She managed to contain her annoyance because if she had retaliated as she wanted to do it would have upset her father. Lester seemed to be aware of the struggle she was having with her temper because his look of amusement broadened into a mocking grin.

Roland looked from one to the other and in an attempt to prevent a breach of the peace, he asked, 'Couldn't he go to law—take out an injunction to stop you?'

'Let him try,' Lester said again. 'In any case, I've got a suspicion that some of those trees are diseased. I've inspected the elms closely—you know that in some parts of the country there's an epidemic of Dutch Elm disease?' Roland nodded. 'Well, I suspect the elms in those woods have got it. If they have, then they'll have to come down in any case, and the sooner the better, before the disease spreads.' He turned to Elise. 'Tell that to your wonderful Phil Pollard. He can protest as much as he likes, but if those elms have got the disease, as I suspect, down they'll come, and fast.'

Harold Lennan looked placatingly at his daughter. 'So there it is, Elise. Building or no building, your precious woods are doomed. You'll just have to find somewhere else

43

to walk, won't you?' He sighed. 'I suppose people have to have houses to live in, and we must all make some sacrifices so that they can have them.'

'I don't agree,' Elise answered, 'there are fields belonging to the estate.' She looked at Lester. 'Why can't you limit your building to them?'

'I've already explained why. The woods cut right across them.'

She collected the empty cups and clattered them together on the tray. 'I still don't see why you can't leave the woods there to—to act as a windbreak or something.'

Lester did not reply. He seemed to be holding on to his patience with difficulty.

She went into the kitchen to wash the crockery and a few minutes later Lester put his head round the door.

'Goodnight, Elise, my little *friend*,' he said. She didn't answer.

He shrugged, made a wry face at Roland and went home.

Elise told Phil Pollard next morning, 'It's true about the woods. Kings are going to cut them down. I had it straight from the "horse's mouth"—Lester Kings himself.'

'So they've made up their minds, have they?' Elise had the impression that he was mentally pulling up his sleeves ready for action.

'Right. We'll call a public meeting and get some posters put up in strategic positions in the town advertising it. The printer down the road will run a dozen or so off quickly, if I ask him nicely.'

So, while Clare dealt with the customers—trade was never very brisk in the mornings—Elise helped Phil to design a poster.

'We must hold it soon,' Phil said. 'I don't trust that old rascal Kings not to do something behind our backs. We've got to give ourselves time to take whatever action we decide on at the meeting.'

'It's not only the old man we're dealing with,' Elise pointed out. 'His grandson's just as ruthless. He said last night he's determined to go through with it. He tried to justify his decision by telling us some tale about the trees having a disease and having to come down anyway.'

'All bluff,' Phil snorted. 'Don't you believe a word of it. But it means we've got even less time than I thought. Now,' he counted on his fingers, 'let's say a day to get the posters printed, another day to distribute them—it won't take long for the grapevine to work...'

'Let's say five days from now,' Elise suggested. 'That brings us to Saturday afternoon.' Phil nodded. 'Where shall we hold it—in the woods?'

'A good idea. Right on the spot. Then people will get the feel of the place and realise just what it is they're protesting about.'

Next morning the posters were ready. Phil put one up in the shop and another in the window. Then he drove round the town handing them out to his fellow shopkeepers, keeping one back to display in his window at home and giving one to Elise who promised to do the same.

Roland protested when he saw the poster in the sitting-room window. 'You can't leave that up, Lester's a friend of ours.'

'Yours, not mine,' she corrected.

'When he comes to the house he'll see it. What am I to say to him?'

'Deny all responsibility. Blame it on me. If he tackles me about it, I'll have my answers ready.'

But Lester did not tackle her about it. In fact they didn't even meet. Whenever he came to see Roland she raced upstairs and locked herself in her room. She persuaded herself that she was not running away from him—she was doing it for the sake of peace and quiet.

The day of the protest meeting was grey and chill. The skies were heavy and held no promise of clearing before the

45

meeting was due to start. A reasonable amount of interest had been aroused by the notices and whenever a customer asked about the meeting, Phil would spend a lot of time persuading them to add their voices or at least their names to the protest.

'The bigger the demonstration,' he said to them, 'the more Alfred Kings and his grandson will take notice.'

Soon after lunch the rain began, a fine soaking rain that seemed determined to continue until nightfall and beyond. Elise put on her raincoat and tied her plastic hood over her hair. She pulled on her boots and raked around in the cupboard for the family umbrella. Roland met her in the hall.

'Coming?' she asked hopefully.

He laughed disparagingly. 'You're playing a losing game. Do you think Lester doesn't know how to deal with this sort of thing? He's experienced it before. He told me last night he has his methods.'

'He'd be surprised at the strength of local feeling,' Elise retorted, irritated by her brother's casual attitude. 'If he's got any sense, he'll change his mind about cutting down those woods. Alfred Kings' reputation in these parts isn't very good as it is, so what it will be like if he goes through with it, I hate to think.'

Roland shrugged. 'Enjoy yourself. At least it's roused you from your customary apathy. It's got you out of your bedroom and away from your precious hi-fi and brought you down to earth.' He looked at her boots. 'Literally.'

She snorted. 'Thanks for your support, brother.' She opened the front door. 'If your wonderful friend Lester wasn't involved, you'd be out there with the rest of us.'

He merely shrugged again and said, 'Shut that door. The wind's freezing cold.'

Elise swept out into the pouring rain and huddled into her coat. Phil was giving her a lift from the end of the road and she got into his car thankfully.

'Hope this rain doesn't put people off,' he muttered,

peering through the rain-spattered windscreen.

There was a small group of people under the trees when they arrived, trying in vain to get some protection from the bare boughs. Elise opened her umbrella and held it over an elderly lady who was standing under a tree, shoulders hunched forward, hands clasped one over the other and stamping her feet.

They talked about the weather. 'What a pity,' the old lady said, 'there are such people as Alfred Kings in the world who go round cutting down beautiful things.'

Elise agreed and looked about her, seeing the great gaunt trees reaching high overhead towards the black clouds, their branches bare of leaves, doomed probably never to see another spring. In that moment of truth, she had to admit to herself that this little protest meeting would make not one atom of difference to Lester and his grandfather. They would find a way somehow of defying the wishes of the local residents.

The people were trickling in instead of coming in their dozens as she and Phil had hoped. Ten minutes later, while the pouring rain beat down on to the carpet of last year's leaves, Phil Pollard began to talk. He spoke fluently and convincingly and he had the crowd with him from the start.

But it troubled Elise to think that he was after all only preaching to the converted—if these people had not agreed with him in the first place, they would not have come.

There was a disturbance on the edge of the crowd and a group of youths started a scuffle. Phil Pollard, disregarding the rain that ran off his hair and down his cheeks, pushed through the crowd and said to the young men, 'If you disagree with what I'm saying, tell me in a civilised way so that I can answer your criticisms.' But they said no, they didn't disagree, they liked the woods as much as he did. It was just that they thought they saw an apprentice from Kings hiding in the crowd and acting as a spy, but admitted they had been wrong.

It was growing dark when Phil resumed his speech. Elise looked round and saw with surprise that most of the crowd were still there. She recognised a familiar figure standing by one of the trees and caught her breath.

What was Lester doing there? He glanced her way, but not a flicker of recognition passed across his face, which was as stiff and cold as a mask.

Didn't he realise, she wondered with a spurt of anxiety, although she chided herself afterwards for allowing it, that if some of the people around them—especially those young men—recognised him as being part of the Kings' set-up, they might attack him? Then—she asked herself in agony —whose side would she be on? She would not allow herself even to contemplate having to make such a choice.

The meeting was unanimous in deciding to consult a solicitor and get advice on the best way to stop the builders from touching the woods until there had been a public enquiry.

The crowd drifted back to the road, where the cars which had brought them were revving impatiently. One by one they pulled out from the kerb and drove away.

Phil took Elise home. 'Good meeting,' he observed as they went along. 'That should give Alfred Kings something to think about. By the way, didn't I see his grandson hovering under one of the trees? What was he doing there— spying on us?'

'Probably,' Elise said bitterly. 'I expect he'll report back to his grandfather about what was said and the decision we came to.'

That evening Elise was doing the washing-up with her father's help when the phone rang. Mr. Lennan answered. The conversation was brief.

'Yes, she's here,' Elise heard him say, then he put the phone down. He returned to the kitchen frowning.

'That was Lester. He seemed annoyed about something. He's coming to see you straight away.'

48

Elise tried to ignore the chill of fear which ran down her spine, and shrugged carelessly. 'It's probably about the meeting this afternoon.'

'How did it go?' her father asked.

She told him what they had decided and he said he sympathised but it was just one of those things, wasn't it? She grew a little irritated with him for refusing to allow himself to get personally involved with anything these days.

He said, in a defeatist tone, 'You won't change Alf Kings' mind, you know. Whatever happens he always goes ahead and does what he wants. He's got a name for it round here. And Lester's no different.'

Elise had reached the landing when the doorbell rang. She stiffened with fright. 'Roland,' she called, 'answer the door.'

But he said, 'You go. I'm busy. It's probably Lester. Tell him I'll be down in a few minutes. You'll have to entertain him until I come.'

Entertain him? Elise would have laughed if she had not felt so afraid. The bell pealed again and she forced her legs to take her down the stairs, one reluctant step at a time, to answer it. As soon as she opened the door, Lester stepped inside. His face was white with anger and as she turned to dive up the stairs his hand shot out and caught her.

'Don't run away,' he said in a tone that frightened her. 'I want to talk to you.'

He pulled her into the sitting-room, closed the door and stood with his back against it, cutting off all means of escape.

CHAPTER IV

'IF it's about the meeting, Lester,' Elise said plaintively, hating herself for her timidity, 'see Phil Pollard. He——'

'It's not about the meeting,' he said through his teeth. 'It's about what happened as a direct result of the meeting.'

She frowned and pushed her hair back uncertainly. She said, shaking her head, 'Then I know nothing about it.'

'Oh, don't you? Are you trying to tell me that you and your precious boss didn't talk that pack of young hooligans into going round to my grandfather's house and hurl stones at the office windows and break them systematically one by one?'

She said, appalled, 'No, of course not. You were at the meeting. You heard what was said. You know we didn't do anything of the sort.'

'I'm not saying it happened in the course of the meeting. I'm saying you spoke to them—bribed them, probably— afterwards, as the crowd left.'

'You really think we would stoop as low as that?' She shrugged. 'All right, think away. You're so unscrupulous yourself you think everyone is the same. But I assure you, we don't use your methods or your grandfather's.'

She could see her words had increased his anger rather than convinced him of her innocence. She sighed. 'I can only repeat that I was not responsible for what those young men did, nor was Phil Pollard. But,' her head came up, 'I have every sympathy with them. I wish I'd thought of it myself. I might even have gone with them and cheered them on.'

Roland pushed at the door and Lester moved to let him in. He had heard her remark.

'Don't be stupid, Elise,' Roland said, plainly worried by his friend's grim expression. 'You know you wouldn't dream of doing such a thing.'

50

She rounded on him. 'Oh, wouldn't I? Why not? Go on, say it—I haven't got the guts! I know what you think of me.' Her eyes swung to Lester. 'And I know what you think of me. And you're wrong, so wrong. It amuses you to call me a mouse—it only shows how little you know about me. I've got my own share of guts and I'm warning you, if you go ahead and tear down those trees, I'm not going to be held responsible for what might happen to any houses you may build where those woods now stand.'

She pushed past her brother and swept up the stairs, leaving behind two astonished men.

As usual after Sunday lunch, she went upstairs to her room next day and put on her headphones. But it was useless, she couldn't concentrate on what she was listening to. She put aside the pile of records, pulled on some slacks, put on her dark blue anorak and called to her father that she was going for a walk.

She made for the woods, over the railway line and up the hill. The path through the woods was churned into mud by yesterday's downpour. The horses' hoofmarks imprinted in the earth by the early morning riders were rain-filled to the brim.

The earth squelched underfoot and Elise wished she had remembered to wear her boots. Hands in her pockets, she wandered beneath the trees, their branches an interwoven canopy of black lines against the sky.

She passed through the fresh-smelling undergrowth, breathing in the heady scent of the soaking leaves. She wondered, as she walked, how she could make Lester change his mind. If she reminded him of how, in childhood, they used to come to these woods, climb the trees, and eat their sandwiches, sitting with their backs to the hard, rough trunks, would he listen with greater sympathy to her pleas? Would she be able to touch his compassion and persuade him to allow the place to remain untouched?

She stood at the side of a holly bush and remembered

51

how the three of them used to gather the scarlet berries at Christmastime and carry them home in triumph to decorate their houses.

She wandered round, naming the trees. Here was a rowan, sturdy and straight; there a birch, its branches thin and graceful even at that time of the year. There was the beech they used to climb and the oak they used to swing on. And this was the hornbeam she had got stuck in and Lester had had to rescue her from its widespreading boughs. There were elms too, the ones Lester had declared were diseased, but to her inexperienced eye, there seemed to be nothing wrong with them.

A mist was coming down now, giving the place a gentle mystery, lending a drifting ghostliness to the trees as though they had already died and were part of the past. The birdsong was faint and twittering as though the birds were apprehensive, sensing the approach of darkness and destruction.

She shivered and made for home, turning for a last look. Her heart thudded as she thought she saw the figure of a man walking between the trees. His head was down and he seemed to be wandering about as she had done, getting the feel of the place and walking among memories. But even as she looked the illusion faded into the mist. She sighed, chided herself for imagining things and went home.

Lester came that evening. Elise was reading and he walked across the room and sat on the arm of her chair. She couldn't bear him so near and started to rise, but his hand restrained her.

He was in a cynical mood, she could sense it. 'How's the brave, fearless, intrepid Elise Lennan this evening? The girl with guts, as she claimed so confidently yesterday, the little mouse that's turned into a great and dangerous tigress.' He put his fingers under her chin and turned up her face. 'If I sit here much longer will she tear me apart with her jaws?'

Elise jerked her chin away. 'Oh, shut up!' she snapped rudely, thinking he would move away. But he stayed where he was.

She looked up at him suspiciously. 'What are you aiming to do—soften me up, talk me round to your way of thinking, and agree with you that the woods should be slaughtered in the name of progress?'

He moved to stand in front of her, the better, she was sure, to drive home his derision. 'Talk *you* round? An insignificant nobody like you? I wouldn't waste my breath.'

Yes, I was right, she thought, he's ridiculing me again, the big brother's friend, superior in his manliness, arrogantly putting the timid little mouse in her place.

'Thanks, Lester,' she said, keeping her eyes down, 'that's just the sort of compliment I've come to expect from you over the years.'

Why did his taunts always have to land dead on target? Why did he always set out to hurt her? And why did she let him?

She gave her attention to the magazine, trying to ignore him as he stood there, hands as usual deep in pockets, staring down at her.

'What are you reading?'

Startled by his change of tone, she looked up. He sounded softer, kindlier, indulgent almost, like a big brother suddenly realising his little sister had feelings and was human after all. And he was smiling.

Caught off guard, she told him. He moved to her side and looked down at the magazine. 'All about hi-fi? You, a girl, trying to understand the technicalities of audio equipment?'

'Why not?' She was on the defensive as usual. 'It helps me to explain it better to customers when I'm selling them the stuff.'

'How incredibly conscientious!' It was a statement spoken with sincerity, without a trace of sarcasm. She

53

flushed at the first real compliment he had ever paid her.

Roland came in and Lester said, 'Your sister will soon be so knowledgeable about hi-fi she'll be able to open a shop of her own.' They laughed. 'I'll have to patronise Phil Pollard's establishment one day and test her knowledge. If I do, Elise, I promise to be the most awkward customer you've ever had!'

Roland invited him to sit down, but he said he would rather stand. He seemed restless and roamed round the room. He stopped with his back to the curtains and looked at his watch, as though he had just come to a decision.

'Do you mind, Roland, if I phone Nina? I haven't heard from her lately and I'd like to know why.'

'She's probably busy, Lester,' Roland said, seeking an explanation which might allay his friend's anxieties. 'You know how hard nurses have to work.'

'All right, so she's busy, but hell, she is engaged to me, after all!'

Roland indicated the phone in the hall. 'It's all yours.'

Elise went upstairs. She could not bear to listen to Lester talking to the girl he was going to marry.

She sat on the bed, reading. She tried to shut out Lester's voice, but he was talking so loudly and so insistently she could not help hearing.

'Yes,' he was saying, 'I know you told me you were seeing a lot of him, but I assumed it was in the course of your work. After all, nurses surely come into contact with doctors all the time——'

There was a pause while he listened, then, 'But why didn't you tell me you were going out with him? You didn't want to upset me? That's rich! All right, so you want to break off the engagement. Go ahead. Consider it an accomplished fact. Send me the ring back? No, *thanks*, keep it as a memento of my love!'

The receiver was slammed down and there was a deep and deathly silence. What should she do? Elise wondered.

Go down to him? Sympathise? No, that she could not do. She stood at the door, uncertain and hesitant.

She heard Roland say gently, 'Come in here, old chap. I'll get you a drink. No, not in there. Elise might come down.'

A door closed and Elise retreated into her bedroom. She sat, staring at the carpet, seeing nothing. There was a murmur of voices from the room beneath her, broken now and then by long, painful silences.

She realised after a while that it was getting late. She had to go down, she couldn't avoid it. Her father would be expecting his cup of tea. She passed his bedroom where he was working and crept down the stairs. It was so quiet, she decided that Lester must have gone.

She opened the sitting-room door and stopped in her tracks. He was standing there, alone, staring hopelessly into the dying fire. She backed out, but he called to her, his voice grating and harsh, 'Oh, come in, for God's sake, and stop creeping around like a bloody little mouse.'

She went in because after that she had no alternative. His shoulders were slouching, his breathing heavy, his eyes bitter with pain.

She ventured, 'I'm so sorry, Lester——'

He rounded on her. 'Don't give me your pity. What do you know about it? You, with your scampering mouse personality. You know nothing, and never will.' He raised his voice. 'And stop looking at me as though I'd suffered a bereavement!'

Roland came in and looked from one to the other. He saw his sister's pale face and his friend's angry eyes.

Elise sank into a chair. She told herself, desperate to check the tears, 'He's been hurt beyond reach or help. That's why he's hurting me. There's no other reason.'

He went on in the same hard tone, 'I've only been ditched by a girl, nothing worse. There are plenty more women around I can enjoy myself with.' He moved in front

55

of her. 'You, for instance. You hurt me once, marked me for life, in fact. Why shouldn't I repay the compliment and leave my mark on you for life?'

He caught her wrist to drag her out of the chair, but she cowered away from him.

Roland said, 'Lester, old chap . . .'

Lester dropped her wrist and sank into the other arm-chair, covering his eyes with his hand.

Elise looked at him with a compassion so strong it drained her of vitality and left her limp. She wanted to comfort him with her body, hold his head against her . . . She reeled under the impact of the feeling, but it passed and she was left sick with fright at what it meant.

Roland motioned her out of the room. 'But, Roland——' she protested softly.

'Oh, let her stay,' Lester muttered. 'Don't worry, I won't touch her. As from this moment on, women, as far as I'm concerned, are poison, strictly not to be taken in any shape or form.'

Roland said pointedly, 'Elise, I've put the kettle on. Make some tea, will you?'

When she got to the kitchen she found she was shaking. With difficulty she pulled herself together and made the tea. Roland took two cups into the sitting-room. Elise gave one to her father and drank her own in her bedroom. Some time later, she heard Lester leave.

Clare was alone in the shop next morning when Elise arrived.

'Hallo,' she said cheerfully, 'Mr. Pollard's just phoned to say he's off to one of the other branches this morning to see a sales rep who's calling there. He's left you in charge.'

Elise had never felt less like being in charge in her life. She had slept badly and even when she had managed to lose consciousness, Lester's face, drawn and miserable, had haunted her dreams. Had he really been so much in love

56

with Nina, who was so many years his junior? Or was it only that his pride had been deeply hurt by the manner of her rejection?

She went into the office, hung up her coat and removed the cover of the typewriter. She typed until coffee time, leaving Clare to serve the handful of customers who called in.

It was while Elise was washing the cups in the little kitchen at the back that she heard a woman customer talking excitedly to Clare. Leaving the crockery to drain, she went to the door of the office and listened. What she heard stunned her so much she went straight into the shop.

The customer turned to her. 'Isn't it awful,' she said, 'have you heard—they're cutting down Dawes Hall woods!'

Elise paled. 'How do you know?'

'I live just past the turning,' she said, 'and you'd have to be deaf not to hear the racket they're making. Without any warning, too. There's been a lot of people protesting about it, did you know?'

Dazed, Elise nodded. 'I was one,' she answered, and added slowly, 'but it doesn't seem to have done much good, does it?'

'It's old Alfred Kings again. Can't trust the old so-and-so,' she commented, picking up the batteries she had bought and taking the change which Clare was handing to her.

'I can guess why he's done it,' Clare said, 'to forestall any trouble from lawyers and so on. Didn't Mr. Pollard say he was going to try to get a solicitor to issue an injunction to stop the builder from doing anything pending a public enquiry?'

'Clever old devil,' the woman snorted as she went out of the door. 'Trust him to think of a way round it.'

Clare looked at Elise. 'Don't take it so hard! The world hasn't come to an end just because they're cutting down a few trees.'

Elise shook her head. She couldn't explain even to Clare,

57

whom she was beginning to trust as she had trusted no other woman, what it meant to her to hear that those particular trees were being chopped down.

She looked at her watch. 'At lunchtime,' she promised herself, speaking aloud, 'I'm going to have a look.'

'The woman could have been wrong,' Clare said soothingly. 'She only heard a noise.'

'I wish you were right, Clare, but something tells me you aren't. If you had seen the mood Lester Kings was in last night . . .' She shook her head. 'At the moment, he's capable of anything,' she nearly added, 'even murder,' but restrained herself.

'Tell me more,' Clare said, intrigued.

'Well, I don't know whether I should tell you, but keep it to yourself'—Clare promised that she would—'he spoke to his fiancée on the phone last night, and she ended the engagement.'

A shadow of pain passed across Clare's face as if the thought of another's suffering stirred memories of her own lost love. 'Then I know how he feels,' she said quietly.

But Elise could not see it that way. She could think only of his savage words, his renunciation of all women from that moment on, his dismissal of her sympathy when she had offered it. She could not be as generous as Clare towards him, not now, not when he was coldly and cruelly massacring the woods which had been part of her life since childhood and which held so many memories of bright untroubled summer days.

At lunchtime Clare said, 'You go, Elise. I can see you can't keep your mind off those woods. I'll hold the fort until Mr. Pollard comes back.'

Elise gave her a grateful smile and went on her way. She walked quickly, her heart pounding with effort and anxiety. She crossed the railway line and as she trod up the hill, she heard the noise the woman had been talking about.

There was the whine of the machinery, the revving of the

58

contractor's lorries, the raised voices of men trying to communicate above the din. She passed the ruins of the old house and came upon the entrance to the woods.

There was a series of shouts, a groaning sound as if someone was dying, a rending and a splitting as a great trunk seared the air, met the ground and bounced a little, like a body falling from a great height. Then it lay still, severed and dead.

She clutched at her scarf with frenzied fingers, her eyes staring, her breath short and panting. Nearby lay two more giants, prostrate and beyond help, broken off near the base, with only the stumps left to show where they had stood. There were young trees, dynamited and blown whole out of the ground, their roots, torn from the earth, reaching hopelessly upwards like supplicant arms, begging to be spared.

She watched, gasping, as a powered chain saw was placed against the trunk of a great beech. The high-pitched whine of the machinery as it started up filled her with a nameless dread, as though she was the one about to be cut down. She winced as the teeth of the saw cut a short way into the bole of the tree. Into the opposite side of the trunk, two men drove steel wedges and swung great hammers to force them home, and she felt the blows as though they were hitting her own body.

Her eyes turned aghast towards the sound of chopping. Her throat grew dry, her lips parched as it came to her what those men were doing. They were hacking at the branches of the hornbeam—the one she had got trapped in when Lester had brought her down. *They were going to fell the hornbeam!*

She became aware of voices nearby, but she did not wait to identify them. She made a convulsive movement forward, her legs advancing of their own accord. She had to stop those men, she had to stop them killing that tree!

She shrieked above the din, 'Stop, *stop*!' and rushed towards them.

59

There was a shout, but she disregarded it. She was in a fever of agony, she had to save the life of that tree . . .

Footsteps pounded behind her, an arm shot out and gripped her shoulder, swung her round and forced her to be still.

'What in God's name do you think you're doing?' Lester shouted, his face white, his lips taut with anger and something else besides. 'Do you want to kill yourself? Don't you know you're as good as committing suicide if you go in there now?'

He pulled her roughly towards the edge of the woods, but she shouted, 'I don't care!' and struggled to free herself.

'Murderer!' she screamed. 'You're slaughtering those trees, you're killing them, one by one . . .' She shook herself out of his hold, and dived among the trees again, hysterical now and out of control.

There were shouts, warning shouts and a pounding of feet. An arm hooked itself chokingly round her neck and she was pulled backwards brutally and swung round and her head pushed down against a hard masculine chest. There was the rending sound again, the groaning and the splitting and the great unbearable thud as another tree hit the ground.

She heard the pounding of Lester's heart beneath her ear, felt the cruel force of his hand on her head. Then he released her and his anger was at white heat. He shouted to the men to hold everything. Then he caught her face between bruising fingers and looked her straight in the eyes, compelling her to look at him.

'You will get—off—this—site, Elise, and you will stay—off—this—site. So help me, if you don't, and if I so much as catch you hanging around even on the fringes of these woods while this operation is in progress, as sure as I stand here I'll call the police and have you arrested! Do you hear me?'

She did not answer. His hands went to her shoulders and

he shook her, trying to make her reply, to show that she understood what he was saying. '*Do you hear me, Elise?*'

She made herself nod. He let her go and her head flopped forward like a new-born baby's, as though it was too heavy for her neck to support. She raised it with difficulty and stared at him as if she had never seen him in her life before. In his safety helmet, in his navy belted working jacket and his thick rubber boots with the trouser legs tucked into the tops of them, he looked a stranger, a cold, ruthless stranger.

She walked away and began to sob uncontrollably. When she reached the bend in the road, she turned for a last look. He was standing there still watching her and her heart leapt at the sight of him.

She walked on until the woods, and Lester, disappeared from view. The sound of machinery faded away and all was as quiet as before. As she made her way home she told herself that it was the trees she had been weeping for, although in her heart she knew it was for Lester, too.

She sat as usual in her room that evening making a determined effort to read, but she could not keep her mind on her book. She had tried listening to her records, but she hadn't heard a note. She was agitated and uneasy, apprehensive in case Lester came.

She had asked Roland if he expected him, but he had been non-committal. 'He might,' was all he would say.

When the doorbell rang, she felt a shock as though she had touched a live wire and got the full force of the mains.

She heard Lester ask, 'Where's your sister?'

'Upstairs,' was the answer.

'Right,' Lester said in a tight voice, and his footsteps took the stairs two at a time.

He walked straight in. She lifted her head sharply and looked at him. Useless to remonstrate with him, to tell him he should have asked permission, useless to say, 'This is my room. Go out.' He was there and had to be faced.

'Well?' he said. That was all. But it was enough.

She was silent, hoping he would go, but he stayed. She knew she had to find an answer. Her eyes faltered and fell away from his, but her words and her tone were belligerent.

'If you think I'm going to say I'm sorry, then you'd better think again.' Her head came up and she challenged, 'You're the one who should apologise.' His eyebrows rose, partly in scepticism, partly in query. She bit out, 'For the slaughter you instigated and were party to. For killing those trees.'

'Oh. So I'm a murderer now, in addition to all my other "virtues". Thanks.' She looked away. 'Tell me,' he said, thrusting his hands into his pockets and lounging against the wardrobe, 'what did you have in mind to do this morning? Stage a sit-in? Do a melodramatic suffragette act and chuck yourself under the wheels of one of the contractor's lorries? Or sit in the middle of it all until a tree crushed you—thus committing the final, noble, heroic act?'

She said through her teeth, 'I should have known you'd be cynical.' She stared at him, simmering. 'The trouble with you, Lester Kings, is that you've got no feelings, no heart, no sentiment. You're insensitive, ruthless and selfish.' She was breathing hard, searching her mind for more derogatory adjectives with which to describe him.

'Go on,' he said, 'it does me no end of good hearing your high opinion of me. Makes me really big-headed.'

'All right, I will. No wonder your girl-friend jilted you. If I'd been in her shoes, I'd have done the same. You're cold, hard and callous!'

He walked towards her slowly. 'That's enough! Let's get one thing straight. You're never likely to be in her shoes. No woman is ever going to be allowed to come that close to me again. Especially you.' She could not raise her eyes and let him see the pain in them.

62

'You take delight in hurting people,' she mumbled, her attack petering out, 'especially me.'

'What do you think I should do to a woman who can't let a day go by without telling me she hates me? Throw my arms round her neck and tell her I love her?'

Hate you? she thought. If only you knew, Lester, if only you knew.

'Let me tell you something, Elise. I've got feelings all right, and I've got a heart, what my beloved ex-fiancée has left of it. Do you think I enjoyed standing there and seeing those trees go down? Do you think I have no memories of the place, and that when I see the trees falling one by one, I don't feel that part of me is going with them?'

'But, Lester,' she whispered, 'why ... ?' Then she remembered. 'Yesterday afternoon, was it you I saw in the woods—in the mist ... ?'

His tension left him and he looked down, pushing up the pile of the carpet with the toe of his shoe. 'Yes. I saw you there, too. I didn't speak to you. I wanted to be on my own, as I guessed you wanted to be.'

'Then, Lester,' she pleaded, hope flooding through her, 'if you feel like that, why can't you stop——'

'Out of the question.' He straightened up. 'My grandfather owns the land. My grandfather decrees that houses are to be built there. I'm working for him, so I follow his instructions. In any case,' his tone altered, became resigned, 'let's face it, if Kings weren't building there, then someone else would come along and do just that. The place was doomed.'

'But, Lester, for the sake of the past ...'

'Sorry.' His attitude had hardened again. She knew she had lost. 'There's no room for sentiment in business. The past is gone, Elise. It's the future that matters now. People need houses, we've got to give them the houses they need.'

He was standing there, looking down at her, so near she could touch him. Yet, in reality, he was beyond reach.

63

'Go on, say it. You hate me.'

He was goading her again and it set her teeth on edge.

'All right, I hate you.'

He walked across to the chair, picked up the doll he had given her years before and thrust it in front of her. 'Pull that apart. Tear it limb from limb. Imagine it's me. Go on, get it out of your system. It'll do you the world of good.'

She saw his baiting smile. He wandered to the door. She raised the doll to throw it at him, but he moved quickly and put the door between them. She hurled the doll all the same and it hit the wood panelling and dropped to the floor, the limbs splayed out supplicatingly like a fallen tree.

She ran across the room, picked up the doll, shook it savagely, then stopped, stared at it, at the pink and white gingham dress, grubby with age, at the blank appeal in the sightless eyes. Then with a despairing movement she lifted it and pressed it lovingly against her cheek.

CHAPTER V

ELISE saw little of Lester for the next few weeks. She made a point of staying in her bedroom whenever he visited the house, and he never came to seek her out as he used to do.

After his warning, she had not dared to return to the woods. Whenever she tried to remember them as they used to be, she only succeeded in visualising the trees as she had seen them for the last time, mutilated, like bodies slaughtered in a massacre.

Whenever she caught a glimpse of Lester talking to Roland in the house, she longed to ask him what the woods looked like now, but her pride would not let her. She wondered whether he had recovered from his broken engagement. Roland never mentioned it and she did not like to ask him in case he told Lester.

One evening as she stood on the landing she heard him talking about the 'site', so she supposed it was all over and Dawes Hall woods were now a part of history. Her resentment against him returned with even greater strength, as though he and and not his grandfather were the cause of all the trouble.

The depth of feeling he aroused in her whenever he came near, and her hatred of all that he had done in destroying something which had meant so much to her, were creating inside her a conflict that seemed destined never to be resolved while their paths continued to cross. Yet she knew that if he ever went away, part of her would go with him.

His return into her life had in itself changed her. By his very presence he had unwittingly broken down all the barriers she had carefully erected between herself and the world and she knew she could never go back to being the self-sufficient recluse she had been allowing herself to grow into before he came.

When Phil Pollard was told about the cutting down of the trees, he said Alfred Kings had not heard the last of it. He would consult a solicitor, he said. But Elise was sure that in his heart Phil acknowledged that Alfred Kings and his grandson had got the better of him and all the others who had joined with him in protest.

One morning Elise saw Clare looking through a new delivery of records.

'My mouth's watering,' Clare said. 'I'm wishing I had something to make music with. Some of these records are fabulous. Not that my taste's very highbrow. All the same ...' She sighed and sorted them out to put on the shelves.

'Why didn't you tell me?' Elise asked. 'I'd have invited you long ago to come and hear mine.'

'Good heavens, I haven't got your taste for the classics.

Chopin is about as high as I go up the classical music ladder.'

'I've got some lighter stuff among my "heavies", as you would probably call them.' She thought for a moment. 'Are you busy tonight?'

'If you mean busy doing nothing, yes.' She frowned. 'My life these days is one big unexciting blank.'

'Then,' Elise took her up eagerly, 'would you come this evening?'

Clare's eyes were suspicious. 'Are you taking pity on me?'

'Yes,' answered Elise without hesitation, knowing it to be the answer Clare expected.

Clare's face cleared at once and she laughed, her cheerfulness returning. 'It's a deal. What time?'

'Seven o'clock?'

'Right,' said Clare, 'seven it shall be.'

Trade became brisk after that. A woman came in to buy a record for her son. He had told her to listen to it on the headphones, she said, before she bought it. Clare showed her into one of the cubicles and left her.

A man came in to buy a record player and Elise took him upstairs to the hi-fi department and demonstrated one or two models. He bought the second one he heard and she told him she wished all her customers were as easy to please as he was. He went out gratified, saying he would have to go a long way to find someone as patient and knowledgeable as she was and he would call again soon.

Phil, who had heard the customer's comments, said with a laugh, 'You'll soon be getting so big-headed, Elise, I'll have to put up your wages!' He shuffled with agitated fingers through the letters on the desk. 'You—er—wouldn't be free tonight, would you?'

'Sorry, Mr. Pollard, no.'

'Got a date?' he asked, without looking up.

Hearing the sharpness in his voice she took pity on him.

66

'Clare's coming round.'

His smile was tinged with relief as she left him to serve another customer.

At lunch-time, Elise waited for a bus to take her into town. She looked at her watch, thinking the bus was late when a van drew up beside her. 'Kings, Builders,' it announced on the side. Below the name in smaller letters were the words, *Live like Kings in a Monarch house*—the slogan Alfred Kings had adopted years before as an advertising gimmick.

The driver leaned across to the passenger's window. 'Want a lift home, Elise?'

'No, thanks, Lester,' she answered, drawing back from the kerb. 'I'm going into town.'

'So am I, so get in.' He opened the door. Her hesitation was so slight a stranger would not have noticed. Lester did. 'What's the matter, afraid of getting into a car with a strange man?' He was taunting her again and she prickled. 'Don't worry, I'll behave. I've forsworn women, remember.'

She got in and sat stiffly on the seat. The springs in the upholstery had gone and she felt every bump in the road.

'Sorry about the state of the van,' he said, looking down at the mud on the floor. He grinned. 'If I'd known I was picking you up—I beg your pardon,' he said with exaggerated politeness, 'giving you a lift, I'd have got one of the workmen to clean it up.'

She let his teasing pass and asked in a flat tone, 'Has building started yet?'

'No. We're doing the fundamentals first, laying drains, putting down services—gas, electricity and so on—and making the roads. Once they used to do that last, after the houses were built. Now we do it first.'

'Oh,' she said dully. 'Have—have all the trees gone?'

'Not all of them, no.'

'The—the hornbeam?'

'That's gone.' He flicked her a look. 'Sorry. Couldn't be saved. But when the architect was planning the site he managed to keep a few of the trees for decoration. One or two oaks and beeches.' He smiled at the windscreen. 'We reprieved a few to give my friend Elise a pleasant reminder of things past.'

'You're no friend of mine,' she muttered. There was no response and she thought he had not heard, but when she stole a look at him he was frowning.

'Thanks, pal,' he said bitterly. He stopped the van on the outskirts of the town. 'This is as far as I go. Sorry.' He leaned across and opened the door for her.

'But,' she protested, 'it's a long walk from here to the shops.'

'It won't hurt you.'

She got out of the van and slammed the door. 'Next time you offer me a lift,' she said through the window, 'you can stuff it.'

She turned away from his malevolent grin.

Roland was in the hall when Clare arrived that evening. Elise had told him a friend of hers was coming. He had looked surprised.

'Didn't know you had any friends. Male or female?'

'Female, of course,' she had snorted.

'Oh. Just wondered. I thought perhaps Phil Pollard might be making some headway at last.' There the conversation had ended, on an abrasive note.

Now he looked at his sister's friend and a flicker passed across his eyes like a breeze ruffling the calm waters of a lake. His sister noted it.

'Clare,' she said, 'this is my brother, Roland. Roland, my friend Clare Hill.' She added maliciously, '*Mrs.* Hill.'

Roland's eyes went dull, like the eclipse of the sun. 'Oh,' he said, adding formally, 'how do you do?'

Clare, unconscious of the messages passing between

brother and sister, put her hand in his and smiled up at him. 'Please call me Clare.'

'If you like,' he replied, withdrawing into himself. He turned away and went into the dining-room.

'Sorry about my brother's lack of polish,' Elise said loudly, 'but he's a crusty old bachelor. He doesn't know how to treat women.'

The dining-room door banged shut.

Elise showed Clare into her bedroom. Clare looked round appreciatively. 'Is this your hidey-hole? Very nice. I like those curtains.' She walked across and fingered the multi-coloured material. 'Where did you get this stuff?'

'The market,' Elise answered. 'Very cheap for the quality.'

'I must go there some time,' Clare said, and looked at herself in the dressing-table mirror. 'My hair's a mess.' She picked up the comb. 'May I?'

Elise nodded. 'If you don't mind mixing the breed!' She watched Clare combing her long jet black hair. 'Wish mine was that colour.' She lifted up a few strands of her own. 'It's mousey.'

Clare considered her. 'You need a new style. Can I try?'

Before Elise could answer, Clare was combing it back from her face and flicking the ends forward to curl round her chin. 'The next time you wash it, pin it in that position. It suits you much better. And why on earth don't you use a better colour lipstick? Let me see,' she put her head on one side, 'pale pink would suit your complexion, not that awful orangey stuff you put on.' She laughed. 'I'll have to take you in hand, my girl. Now, where are these records?'

They sorted through Elise's collection and put aside a few to be played.

The doorbell rang and Elise jumped. Clare took away the records she was holding. 'You're not safe with that. It's a good job you don't handle records in the shop. You react too violently. Every time the shop doorbell rang you'd drop

69

the record you were holding!'

Embarrassed, Elise laughed. She could not tell even Clare why she had jumped. 'It's a friend of Roland's,' she explained offhandedly. 'Lester Kings.'

Clare stared. '*The* Lester Kings—your arch-enemy?' Elise nodded. 'You mean you have to be sociable to him, feeling all the time you'd like to murder him?'

'Well, that's putting it a little strongly, but . . .'

'I quite understand,' Clare said, laughing. 'Now, let's listen to this one first.'

· They had played all but one of the records Clare had chosen. Now she was listening to the last with the concentration which seemed to come naturally to anyone using stereo headphones. She was staring into the distance, lost to the world, when the door opened.

Lester walked in. With difficulty she focused and stared at him. Then, astonished, she looked at Elise. Her eyes asked, 'How can you let him walk into your bedroom like this without permission?'

Elise frowned at Lester. 'What do you want?'

'Nothing.' He grinned and propped himself against the wall. 'Just a *friendly* visit.' He looked at Clare, who was removing the headphones. 'Sorry to interrupt.'

Clare smiled. 'It's all right.'

He looked at Elise, eyebrows raised. 'Aren't you going to introduce us?'

'Sorry. Clare, this is Lester Kings, a friend of my brother's.' She emphasized the words and Lester's eyes mocked her.

'Lester, this is Clare Hill. She works in the shop,' she added, with the same malice as before, '*Mrs.* Hill.'

But the explanation of Clare's marital status seemed to have no effect on him. He turned on a specially warm smile —Elise thought, 'He's never smiled like that at me'—and took Clare's outstretched hand.

'Another hi-fi fiend, Mrs. Hill?' he asked.

70

Clare shook her head. 'Just frustrated at selling so many records that I can't hear myself. So Elise took pity on me. And please call me Clare.'

'Do thou likewise, Clare. Call me Lester.'

'My word,' Elise thought sourly, 'he's putting on the charm. So much for his claim that he's forsworn women!'

Her sulky expression caught his eye and he moved to sit beside Clare on the bed. 'And how do you like shop assisting?' His gaze moved approvingly over her.

Clare responded to the flattery in his eyes with a grin. 'Fine, just fine.'

Elise turned away. He's flirting with her, she thought, disgustedly. For all he knows, she's a married woman.

'Mr. Pollard's good to work for. Hasn't Elise told you?'

'Ah yes, Phil Pollard.' He leaned back across the bed and supported his head against the wall. 'Elise's boy-friend.'

She swung round. 'You know very well he's not my boy-friend!'

Clare looked from one to the other. 'It's the first I've heard of it.'

'He's not, Clare, really. It's just——'

'It's just that he's got his eye on her,' Lester commented with spite.

'But, Elise,' Clare said, 'isn't he a little old for you?'

'What does that matter in this day and age?' Lester asked with cynicism. 'These days a man's as young as he feels. Isn't he, Elise?' She heard the taunting tone and turned to her friend.

'It's just that—well, he keeps asking me out. But he's not my "boy-friend".' She turned a venomous gaze on to Lester. 'I haven't got one and I don't want one.'

Lester laughed sardonically. 'It would do you the world of good, Elise, my *friend*, to take to yourself a boy-friend.'

Clare looked at him with interest. 'Have you got a girl-friend, Lester?'

His face clouded and cleared as though the cloud had never been. 'No.'

'Then,' she went on brightly, 'what's wrong with you two getting together?'

Elise stared at her and saw the mischief in her grin. How could she let her down like that!

Lazily Lester rose and put his arm round Elise's shoulders.

She tried to twist away, but he held her. 'She hates me,' he said. 'Hardly a day goes by without her telling me so, either by word or deed.'

'But,' Clare pointed out, 'it's always possible for hate to turn into love.'

Lester removed his arm. 'Never.'

'Lester,' Elise said, unable to eliminate the bitterness from her tone, 'obviously believes in the old saying, "once bitten, twice shy". You see, Clare, he's been jilted by the girl he was engaged to.'

Clare said to Lester, her face serious, 'But why should that make you cynical about love? Surely it was better for you to have found her out this side of marriage, instead of afterwards?'

Lester did not respond. His hands were in his pockets and he was leaning against the wardrobe. His face showed no expression at all.

'Love between two people,' Clare went on softly, her eyes groping like someone looking into the misty distance, 'two people who have a deep and permanent relationship, is the most wonderful thing in the world.'

Lester straightened and went out.

'Oh dear,' said Clare, 'I hope I haven't upset him.'

Elise laughed bitterly. 'Nothing could upset him. He hasn't got any feelings to hurt.'

Clare looked at her as though pitying her for her inexperience. 'Take it from me, Elise, men are human, too. They have feelings, just like us. And Lester's no exception.'

Later, Elise took Clare down to the sitting-room while she made a cup of tea for them all. The room was empty and she gave Clare a magazine to read.

Lester came into the kitchen and sat on a corner of the table. 'So you've got yourself a friend?'

'Yes.' She turned on him. 'And there was no need for you to flirt with her. I told you, she's "Mrs." Hill.'

'And I happen to know,' he said, his eyes narrow, 'that she's a widow. My grandfather knew her husband before he died. And that means she's back on the marriage market.'

'What a way to put it,' Elise said disgustedly. 'That's typical of you.'

Lester stood so suddenly the table scraped harshly against the tiled floor. He said savagely, 'Can't you stop criticising me? According to you, everything I do is wrong, wrong, *wrong*!'

He strode out of the kitchen, called to Roland that he was leaving and slammed the front door behind him.

Elise stood rigid, her eyes closed, appalled at what she had done. She could not believe that he was so vulnerable. Had his fiancée's rejection affected him so deeply? Had he still not recovered from his broken love affair? She wanted to run after him and apologise.

Then the pendulum swung and she thought, seeking justification for her unpleasantness to him, 'He's hurt me often enough in the past. I've hurt him for a change. Now he knows what it's like.'

But there was cold comfort in the thought. It came to her like a match being struck in the darkness—the simple truth that when a woman hurts the man she loves, she hurts herself more.

Roland was in the sitting-room when she carried in the tray of tea. He was reading, sullen and silent. 'What's the matter with him?' Elise wondered, feeling sorry for Clare who was trying not to look embarrassed.

When her father came down, he filled the room with his

solid, comforting presence and the tension vanished. He talked to Clare and listened with interest to her replies and the three of them kept the conversation going until Clare went home.

Afterwards, when Roland was drying the crockery, Elise asked casually if he liked her new friend, Clare.

He was noncommittal. 'She's a bit inconsiderate, isn't she?'

'How do you mean——'

'Won't her husband be worried about her staying out so late?'

Elise laughed. She had fooled her brother completely. 'She hasn't got a husband. She's a widow.'

She dived to catch the cup he was drying before it crashed to pieces on the floor.

Next morning, Elise apologised to Clare for her brother's behaviour. 'He's a bit boorish in his attitude to women, I'm afraid.'

Clare shrugged without looking up. 'It's all right.'

'He's heavy going in company. Like his occupation.'

'What's his job?' Clare asked idly.

'He's an accountant. He's a junior partner in a firm on the other side of the town. It's lucrative, but dull.'

Clare nodded without much interest. Elise was puzzled by her offhand manner and went into the office to type answers to the morning's letters.

Clare was washing up the coffee cups when the shop door was thrust open and Roland walked in. Elise, who was standing behind the counter, turned pale. She thought there was something wrong with her father.

'What's the matter?' she asked, putting a hand to her throat.

'Nothing,' her brother answered irritably. Elise relaxed. He peered into the office at the back. 'Is old man Pollard in?'

74

'No. What do you want to see him for?'

'I don't. Where's Clare?'

'*Clare*? In the kitchen, washing up. Why?'

'I want to see her.'

'But, Roland ...'

'Look, Elise, I've got myself half an hour off work. I shouldn't really have come.' He looked at his watch. 'I've got fifteen minutes left and it'll take me over ten to get back.' He repeated, 'Where's Clare? For goodness' sake, have some tact, Elise. I can't explain yet.'

She pointed. 'Through the office, first door on the left.'

He followed her directions. Five minutes later, he hurtled out of the kitchen, through the office, across the shop and out of the door. Just before he shut it, he remembered to wave.

Elise's mouth came open. She couldn't help it. She had never been so staggered in her life. Clare came back, her cheeks pink, her eyes bright.

'Don't tell me if you don't want to,' Elise said, curiosity bursting out of her like stuffing from a torn cushion.

'Of course I want to. He's—he's asked me to go out with him tonight. I said "yes".'

'He's—*what*?' Clare's cheeks turned pinker. 'But Roland never notices women. I didn't think he knew they existed.'

Clare laughed, and it was a happy sound. 'We all know what sisters think of their brothers. But brothers are attracted by other people's sisters, not their own, so it doesn't matter, does it?' She looked anxiously at Elise. 'You don't mind?'

'Mind? Good heavens, no. I—I——' She shook her head, giving up.

Clare laughed again. 'You're speechless. All right, let's leave it at that.'

Elise went back to the office and began to type. She worked mechanically, her mind still numb with shock. Her brother taking a girl out! Roland interested in a woman!

She said the words to herself again and again, but they bounced off like hail on concrete.

Clare, even more cheerful than usual, put her head round the office door. 'Customer, Elise. A man. Asking specially for you.'

'Me? Why me?' She took out her comb and ran it quickly through her hair. If he was asking for her he must be someone important. She snapped her bag shut and went through into the shop.

'Hallo,' said Lester.

It was her second shock of the day, and she felt in need of a chair. Instead she made herself look professional. 'Can I help you?' she asked in her most mincing, shop-assistant tones.

He was leaning on his elbow on the counter and his hands were clasped loosely in front of him. He wore a sardonic grin as he looked her up and down and she noticed he was dressed in working clothes, complete with muddy boots. The only thing that was missing was his safety helmet. She supposed he had left that in the van.

He seemed in cheerful mood. 'The super-efficient counter-hand,' he murmured, and she knew he was aiming to provoke.

He did not change his position. 'Yes, you can help me. And—er—shouldn't you address me as "sir"?'

He saw her lips drawn inwards and her eyes spark like dry tinder burning. He smiled again. 'I've come to buy some hi-fi equipment.'

She controlled her surprise and schooled herself into allowing not a flicker of it to escape. 'It's upstairs. Will you follow me?'

She turned her back on his grin and heard him call out, 'See you later, Clare.'

His booted footsteps thudded behind her up the narrow staircase to the first floor.

'What are you particularly interested in?' she asked,

76

keeping her voice toneless and her expression one of simulated interest.

'Come off your high horse, Elise, and speak to me like a human being instead of a damned efficient robot.' His mouth was smiling, but his eyes were not.

'What are you interested in?' Her tone had not altered.

He said curtly, 'I want a stereo record player, a turntable.'

'You mean a transcription unit?'

He raised his eyebrows at her use of the correct terminology. 'Yes.' He was as businesslike as she was now, and as distant as an ordinary customer. 'What have you to offer? I want something good.'

'Would you be prepared to go into the higher price ranges?' Her voice was strictly formal.

'Within reason, yes.'

She led the way across the room and showed him a turntable displayed on a shelf. 'This is the best one we stock. I know it's good because I've heard it in action.'

'Could I hear it in action?' He looked at her, his eyes those of a stranger. 'Can you demonstrate it for me?'

'Of course. I take it you have an amplifier at home?' He nodded and watched her deft fingers as she connected the turntable to the demonstration amplifier and connected this to two large speakers.

'Clever girl.' She swung round at his changed tone and saw the mockery in his eyes. But there was admiration in them, too. She flushed.

'What would you like to hear—something classical,' she asked sharply, 'or something more popular?'

'You make the choice.'

She chose a Tchaikovsky symphony and he commented, 'I see your musical taste favours the romantics, what with this and *Schéhérezade*.'

'What's wrong with that?' she asked with irritation.

'Nothing. It's just that I thought you had forsworn

romance as I've forsworn women. After all, your way of life could hardly be called romantic, could it?'

She held in her retort as he knew she must and put on the record. The music filled the large room and as she listened, she looked at him covertly. He stood remote and withdrawn, wrapped around in concentration. After a while he indicated that he had heard enough.

'Now I should like to hear one or two more turntables for the purpose of making comparisons.'

She sighed and looked at her watch. She was due to go home to lunch soon. But he was a customer—a valued customer at the price he seemed willing to pay for a piece of equipment—so she had to keep her patience and carry on without protest.

She made a mistake in one of the connections and tutted loudly. He strolled across to her. 'What's the matter? I warned you that if I ever came into your shop, I'd be an awkward customer.'

'You can say that again,' she murmured under her breath. Then, sorry at once for stepping out of line, she looked at him and apologised.

He smiled, reached across and took the screwdriver from her fingers. 'Let me do that.' And he connected the speaker to the amplifier while she watched.

'Thanks,' she said sullenly, refusing to look at him.

It was when she was connecting up the fourth record player that she heard Phil Pollard's voice downstairs. 'Where's Elise?' he was asking Clare.

She looked quickly at Lester. He was frowning. 'Upstairs,' they heard Clare answer, 'demonstrating some equipment to a customer.' Then she lowered her voice thinking they could not hear, 'It's Lester Kings.'

They heard an explosive noise from Phil. 'I'm going up,' he said.

Lester wandered to Elise's side and rested on his elbow against the counter. By the time Phil appeared at the top of

78

the stairs, Lester was gazing into her face with something approaching adoration.

'Stop it,' she hissed, but his lovesick expression did not alter.

'Hallo, Mr. Pollard,' she said, trying to move out of range of Lester's eyes, but the work she was doing effectively prevented it.

'Hallo, Elise,' he said gruffly, looking at Lester with venom.

Lester slowly turned his head to look at Phil, smiled, then as if he could not stand being distracted from his contemplation of Elise for more than a few seconds, let his eyes wander back to her again.

This time his gaze took in more than her face. It pointedly explored the trim figure underneath her pale blue dress and when he heard the heavy breathing of the owner of the shop turn into a gasp of strangled anger, he moved nearer to her.

Phil Pollard fiddled amongst the equipment for a few moments, pretending to be looking for something, then, as if he could not stand it any longer, went downstirs again.

When they were alone, Elise turned on Lester. She opened her mouth to hurl whispered abuse at him, but he raised his hand to caution her, thus in one action reminding her both of his status as a valued customer and her own as a subservient shop assistant.

Another twenty minutes was to go by before he finally made up his mind to take the first turntable she had demonstrated. By that time she felt reduced to the instability and shakiness of a jelly, whereas Lester was as calm and collected as when he had first walked into the shop.

He paid by cheque and loaded the turntable into the van which was parked at the kerb. Then he returned to buy some records.

Thankfully Elise handed him over to Clare and while she served the other customers, was forced to see him laughing,

79

talking and generally making up to the young woman who now appeared to be her brother's girl-friend.

She did battle with her feelings and lost, giving herself up to an orgy of jealousy. When lunchtime finally came, Lester was still in the shop. His back had been turned to the filthy stares the shop owner was directing his way. He knew Phil Pollard could do nothing about his prolonged visit, because he was spending more money that morning than many customers spent in a month.

When Elise went home, she called out 'goodbye' to Phil and Clare but ignored Lester, although he turned at the sound of her voice. She walked past her usual bus stop because the last thing she wanted was to be offered a lift by the grandson of Alfred Kings, although she knew it would have got her home in half the time.

When a Kings' van did cruise along beside her for a few yards and a voice called her name, she turned away to stare into a shop window until the driver swung the van from the kerb and revved angrily and noisily into top gear as he drove away.

Elise was in the middle of washing her hair that afternoon when the phone rang. She clasped the towel round her shoulders and ran downstairs to answer it.

'Elise?' said a voice she knew only too well. 'This is your awkward customer.'

'Oh,' she said. Then, 'What do you want, because I'm in the middle of washing my hair, and it's dripping all over the telephone and carpet.'

He thought that was very funny, he said, and if he wasn't in the site office with half a dozen people queueing outside to see him, he'd keep her talking for half an hour. Then he went on, 'That turntable you sold me this morning——'

'Is there something wrong with it?'

'I wouldn't know,' he came back smoothly, 'I haven't had time to listen to the darned thing yet, have I?' She apologised and said she had forgotten he was a hard-working man these days.

He ignored her sarcasm and continued, 'But I'll be trying it out this evening. Would you like to come along to my place and hear it in action?'

She didn't answer at once. She held her breath.

'Elise—are you still there?'

She let the breath out slowly. 'Of course I am.' She had to make him repeat his question in case she had misunderstood his words. 'Do you mean——'

'I mean I'm inviting you to my digs to listen to the turntable you sold me this morning.' His tone became softer, insinuating. 'What else did you think I had in mind?'

She snapped, 'You know very well that's not what I thought you meant!' She was aware that she was overreacting and was glad of the distance between them to hide her blushes. 'But it's—very kind of you to ask me. What time?'

'I'll call for you about eight. All right?' There was a pause, then, 'Now go and dry your hair and make yourself look beautiful—*if* you can.' He rang off.

She bit her lip. A typical Lester Kings 'farewell' to his old friend's sister!

When Roland came home he said, 'I'm taking Clare out this evening. Did she tell you?'

Elise nodded and her brother's look dared her to comment. She countered his challenge by telling him about her date with his friend. He stepped back like someone who had had a blow aimed at him.

'You're going to Lester's? What on earth for?'

She shrugged. 'Because he invited me.' She did not explain, she maliciously left him to come to his own conclusions—and knew they would be wrong. Instead of looking pleased as she thought he might, he seemed worried. A frown creased his forehead and he ran an uncertain hand through his thick light brown hair.

'I thought he'd finished with girls.'

81

She shrugged again nonchalantly and swaggered up the stairs. But her manner reverted to normal when she was out of his sight.

After their evening meal, Roland went off in his car to collect Clare. Elise had never seen such purpose in his actions, such decision in his movements. This was a side of him that had been kept securely hidden because, she supposed, there had never been any incentive before to bring it into the open.

When Mr. Lennan heard of his children's sudden plunge into the social whirl, he was not disturbed. 'I wonder,' he said, when told of Lester's invitation, 'if he's got over his broken engagement yet?'

Elise told him, 'He said he'd renounced women, so I don't think he has recovered.'

Her father laughed. 'Renounced women? At his age? He'll change his mind. He'll meet some nice girl who'll knock him cold, then he'll wonder what he ever saw in the other one.'

Her father was speaking, Elise mused sadly, as though Lester had not yet met the wonderful creature who would 'knock him cold'. And he hadn't, of course. She knew that her effect on men had always been nil and always would be, especially on Lester.

She wore a dress she had bought for Christmas and had never worn since. It was apricot-coloured, long-sleeved and close-fitting. It buttoned to the neck and had delicate touches of white in the collar, cuffs and belt.

She combed her hair as Clare had done, flicking the ends forward so that they framed her face. She used a little more make-up than usual and slipped her feet into a new pair of white shoes. She changed her possessions into a matching white handbag, then sat on the bed and wondered why she had gone to all that trouble.

It's only Lester I'm seeing, she told herself. What difference does it make how I look?

When she opened the door to him, he stepped inside and stopped dead. 'You are—Elise Lennan?'

She coloured at his meaning—that in his opinion Elise Lennan could never look attractive, no matter how hard she tried.

'I'm sorry, yes, I am.' She closed the door, wanting suddenly to run up to her room and tear it all off. What had made her dress up like this? What would he think—that she was after him?

'I'll get my coat,' she said dully, feeling all the excitement which had buoyed her up all the afternoon drain away.

She called up to her father that they were going and he peered down from the landing and said he hoped they enjoyed themselves.

'We're only going to listen to some music,' she said as they went out to Lester's car. 'I don't know why he said that.'

Lester did not comment. His odd silence made her feel awkward. It could only mean that he was embarrassed by her obvious desire to please him and it was as much as she could do to force herself to get into his car and not run back into the house.

He hardly spoke on the way to his digs, except to comment on the arrival of spring and how the evenings were getting longer.

They met his landlady in the hall and he introduced them. Mrs. Carter, her name was, and she looked Elise up and down appreciatively. Then she glanced at Lester with a knowing light in her eye. He did not appear to notice, and motioned Elise up the stairs.

'First on the left,' he said, and showed her in. 'This is my living-room. The room next door is my bedroom.'

His manner was brisk as he removed some books from the armchair and invited her to sit down. He took off his jacket and threw it on the floor under the window. His shirt was a brilliant yellow and he was wearing a flower-patterned tie, his trousers were deep blue cords, tightly belted at the waist. The effect his careless good looks had on Elise's pulse rate unnerved her. She was so tense that even her thoughts seemed cemented in concrete.

She reached for a book and opened it to hide her shyness. It was a textbook about building. She heard him laugh and realised he was standing beside her chair holding out a glass. She put the book aside and took the drink he was offering.

He sat on the couch, stretching out his long legs and resting his head on a cushion. 'Teaching yourself to become a builder now, as well as a highly efficient saleswoman of audio equipment?' She coloured at his compliment and he went on, 'I was most impressed by the girl who served me—so patiently and knowledgeably—this morning.' He studied the contents of his glass. 'If she hadn't swept out of the shop in such a huff at lunchtime and in addition refused the lift I offered her, I would have told her so earlier.'

She shrugged, trying to look as though his praise meant nothing to her. 'It's my job.'

Through the long silence that followed, she tried to think of something to talk about, sifting through her thoughts like a detective seeking evidence of a crime, but could not find a single clue to help her.

He did not seem to be bothered. He even closed his eyes. She wanted to cry out, 'Look at me, acknowledge I'm here, don't ignore me as if I didn't exist!'

What would he be doing, she wondered, torturing herself with her own incoherence and inadequacy, if I were attractive and interesting and full of charm?

He said, without opening his eyes, 'So Roland's got himself a girl-friend?'

'How did you know?' she asked, her voice coming out strange and thin.

'He rang me at the site office in case I was going round to

see him tonight.'

So Lester had filled in the evening, had he, by inviting her to his place, an evening which would otherwise have been long and boring and lonely. He must have decided that even her company was preferable to his own.

'He seems rather keen on her,' he remarked casually.

'Yes.' She frowned. 'I can't understand it.'

He laughed loudly and opened his eyes. 'Now is that statement a product of your ignorance of the facts of life? Or is it that you're casting doubts on Clare's attractiveness, or is it surprise that your brother is at last displaying signs of becoming aware of the fascinations of the opposite sex?'

She smiled back at him. 'The third, I think.'

'Unbelievable,' he said, watching her, 'that all that masculinity has been sleeping below the surface, undisturbed for years. Then a pretty young woman comes along and without even trying, wakes it roughly from its slumbers, and he's up and after her like an animal in search of a mate.'

She acknowledged his words with a smile, but said, 'What puzzles me is that they hardly addressed a word to each other.'

He leaned forward, resting his elbows on his knees and clasping his glass between his palms. 'My dear girl,' he said softly, 'it's obvious, whatever you may say to the contrary, that you don't know the facts of life.' She started to protest. 'You may think you do, but,' he shook his head, 'as far as sex is concerned you're ignorant, untutored and if I may say so, utterly unawakened.'

She hunched herself up in the chair and turned her head away. Why was he talking like this? When would he stop his probing and stop torturing her with the truth?

'You need a boy-friend.'

Her head shot round and there was fear in her eyes. 'No, thank you!'

'I didn't say you *want* one, I said you need one.' He

85

examined her speculatively. 'And I know just the person to suit you.'

Now what was coming? Half in fear, half in hope, she waited.

CHAPTER VI

'THE man's name,' Lester said slowly, 'is Howard Beale.'

She turned her cheek against a cushion and closed her eyes to hide the pain. What had she expected—a proposal of marriage from Lester Kings?

'He's a surveyor, comfortably off, owns a big car, lives—on his own—in a large detached architect-designed residence.' He paused. 'And he's looking for a woman to share it with him.' He waited for a response but none came. 'Does the idea attract you?' Still no answer. 'I'll arrange a meeting. It shouldn't be difficult to get you together.' She made no movement. 'If your brother has stolen the only friend you've ever had,' he continued relentlessly, 'and what's more, in doing so has found himself a wife, you won't want to be left out in the cold, will you?'

She moved at last, managing to cloak her misery with anger. 'I told you,' she rasped, 'I don't want—or need—a boy-friend. I'm perfectly happy as I am.'

'You look it,' he said cuttingly.

She stood up. 'If this is all you propose to talk about for the rest of the evening, I'd better go.'

He stood too. 'All right, we'll change the subject. Come over here and watch me connect up the expensive new toy you sold me this morning.'

He took a screwdriver from a toolbox and started connecting the wires to the amplifier, then to the two speakers which stood in opposite corners of the room. 'Don't inspect my workmanship too closely, will you? This is just what they call a "lash up" for your benefit. I'll do the job properly when I've got more time.'

She smiled, happier now that the conversation had veered away from personalities to a sphere in which she felt completely at home.

'While I'm doing this,' he said over his shoulder, 'you sort through my new records.'

She did so, exclaiming with pleasure at his choice.

'You mean to say,' he said to the back of the speaker, 'you like my taste in music? There's actually something about me you approve of? My word,' he straightened and put away his screwdriver, 'that surely calls for celebration. Let's drink to it.'

He refilled her glass and put it into her hand. 'Let's drink to the future—to me in my lonely bachelor flat, and you in your architect-designed detached house.'

She took the glass from her lips and started to lower it angrily to the coffee table. He held up his hand. 'All right, let's make it simply—to us.' He raised his glass and touched hers, then he tossed the drink down his throat. She sipped hers and they waited for each other to speak first.

He was frowning into her eyes and seemed to be seeking for something which escaped him, the answer to a question he had not even asked.

'Have you chosen a record?' he said, at last, a little abruptly.

She held one out. 'This. Beethoven. His fifth piano concerto.'

'Better known as the "Emperor".' He slid the record gently from its cover and she watched as he put it on the turntable and switched on.

'I'd better not ask the expert how I'm doing,' he said, 'I might get a rude answer.'

He sat on the couch and patted the cushion at his side. She sat next to him and gave all her attention to the music.

'It's good, isn't it?' he said, after a while.

'Musically or mechanically?' she asked, smiling impishly and deliberately misunderstanding him.

'You know very well I meant mechanically. Musically its goodness goes without saying.' He lifted his hand to ruffle her hair, but pulled it back when she shrank away from him.

They listened again, she with the same concentration, he a little more withdrawn than before.

At the end of the second movement Elise said, 'I'm sure I could detect some distortion.'

'M'm, I was wondering about that myself.'

'I think I know the cure.'

'You do?' He waved his hand towards the record player. 'Go ahead. It's all yours.'

She turned the switch and stopped the turntable. He came to stand beside her, hands in pockets. 'What are you going to do?'

'Adjust the playing weight of the pick-up arm.' She looked up at him. 'Do you mind?'

'Not at all. I bow to a higher authority.' His sarcasm passed over her as she carefully adjusted a small attachment at the side of the playing arm.

'That should do it. I've increased the playing weight by about half a gram.'

'Have you now?' His eyes mocked her, but his smile was indulgent. 'Let's see if it's made any difference.'

The heard the concerto through to the end. 'Excellent,' he commented. 'Not a trace of distortion, was there? Now, how much do I owe the mechanic for her invaluable services?'

'Er—let me see.' She grinned at him. 'My charges are higher outside working hours.'

'Are they indeed? That's a surprisingly provocative statement for such a timid little mouse.' He moved towards her. 'Shall we show her what that sort of provocation does to a man? In her innocence she could hardly know.'

He stood in front of her and began to slide his hands from his pockets. She backed away and jumped violently as someone hammered on the door.

'It's all right,' he said, 'it isn't Fate demanding an entry. It's Mrs. Carter with some refreshments which, judging by your nervous state, you appear to need.'

He opened the door for his landlady and she entered, a tray lifted triumphantly high before her, and lowered it carefully to the coffee table. It was laden with sandwiches and cakes, crockery and a large pot of coffee.

'It's very good of you,' Elise said, overwhelmed by the quantity of food they were expected to eat.

'Not at all, dear,' Mrs. Carter said, her eyes skating round the room and sweeping up and down Elise with the efficiency of a large paintbrush. 'I expect you're hungry by now.'

She winked at Lester and withdrew with a calculating, anticipatory grin.

'I did tell her not to bother,' Lester said, 'but she insisted. She really only did it to inspect the state of the battlefield. Hence her comments about "being hungry" after the strenuous activities she no doubt assumed we've been indulging in.' He told her to sit down and help herself. 'It's the first time I've had a girl here, which accounts for her inspection of you, now and when you arrived. She was endeavouring to discover the state of your morals,' he took a bite out of a sandwich, 'the degree of permissiveness you would allow without first having a ring on your finger.' He took another bite and finished the sandwich. 'She obviously summed you up correctly.' He held out the plate of cakes to Elise and she took one. 'Which accounts for her knowing wink at me. She now regards me as a marked man. She's married me off—to you.'

Elise spilt the coffee as she poured it out and had to search in her bag for a paper tissue to mop it up.

'But there's no need to worry,' he went on. 'I'll disillusion her in the morning. I'll simply tell her I'm not the marrying kind.'

'That,' she said, handing him his coffee and avoiding his eyes, 'sounds even worse. A sort of "love 'em and leave 'em" attitude.'

'And that,' he answered, 'is my maxim, my motto from now on.'

She said steadily, looking into his eyes now, 'There's no need to warn me off, Lester. I'd never dream of putting myself in the category of one of your girl-friends. And I assure you you're the last man I'd ever think of in the role of my husband, *if* I ever took one.'

He was silent, intent on drinking his coffee. After a while he said, 'I'm right, aren't I, in thinking you can type? My grandfather's clerical assistant is going away soon to look after her daughter who's expecting a baby any day now. I was wondering if you would consider helping him out some afternoons, answering letters and so on.' He looked at her, eyebrows raised.

'I suppose I could,' she answered, after thinking about it. 'As long as I have enough time left to do the housework and so on.'

'Good,' he said, 'and thanks. I'll tell him.' After a pause he said, 'Did I tell you that the room my grandfather is having redecorated for me is ready and waiting? I'll be moving in there soon.'

She looked round. 'I suppose it will be more comfortable than this.'

He raised his arms and linked his hands behind his head. 'It certainly will be, in more than one sense of the word. There'll be less supervision.' At her puzzled look he explained, 'No prying eyes of a gossiping landlady to scrutinise my lady visitors. Or how long they stay.'

He saw her ill-concealed irritation and grinned provocatively. 'After I've moved, I can entertain a different girl-friend every night, if I feel so inclined, can't I?'

90

She frowned. 'Your grandfather wouldn't approve of that.'

'Wouldn't he? That's where you're wrong. He measures a man's worth, his standing in life by the length of his list of women friends, by his "way with the ladies" as he would put it. He was no saint when he was young, so he would regard it as a case of "like grandfather, like grandson"!'

She could not hold back her anger. 'I thought you said you'd finished with women?'

He smiled lazily. 'I have—in the singular.'

He watched her jerk herself to her feet and walk across to the new turntable. 'You look as though you covet my new toy.'

She touched it and sighed. 'It's just that I've been wanting something as good as this for a long time, but with Dad having to do so much college work at home and needing peace and quiet, it just isn't possible.'

'It would be odd,' he said at her side, 'if you were my girl-friend. I'd never know who you loved best—me or my record player.'

She did not look at him as he seemed to want her to. She held herself in until he moved away.

'Did Nina like music?'

'Couldn't tell you. I never had a chance to find out.'

'Too busy doing other things, I suppose?' She forced her tone to be disinterested.

He grinned sardonically. 'How did you guess?'

She told herself she had got the answer she deserved.

He searched in the record rack and pulled out a record. 'This is the one I want.' He put it on and poised the stylus over the record. 'Sit down and listen to this.'

As the pure, liquid notes of the piano drifted into the room, her heart throbbed painfully, and she stared at him.

'Recognise it?' he asked softly. She nodded and listened until the music ended, dying away into silence, a questioning silence.

'It was *Für Elise*.'

'Yes. Written by Beethoven for a girl he loved.' He got up. 'His affair with her was sweet—but short.' He replaced the record in its sleeve. 'Like me, Beethoven was used to broken love affairs.'

'How long have you had it?'

He shrugged, 'Years.'

'Why did you buy it, Lester?' Her voice was a whisper.

'Couldn't tell you. Perhaps because it reminded me of a girl I used to know who bit me so badly I've still got the scar.' He smiled and replaced it in the rack. 'It's getting worn out with being played so much.'

Hope lit in her eyes like a candle flame.

'I'll probably throw it out soon,' he muttered. 'It's not worth replacing.'

The flame flickered and died away. 'Thanks for playing it,' she said, her voice toneless, her pleasure gone. 'I'd better go, or you'll be throwing me out.'

He looked at his watch. 'So soon? You'll be disappointing Mrs. Carter.'

'She's doomed to disappointment anyway, isn't she?'

'Don't say it as though the idea upsets you.'

She forced a smile. 'You're not the only one who's not the marrying kind, remember.'

'I begin to think,' he said, going into his bedroom to get her coat, 'that the coffee you drank must have contained some vinegar.'

He helped her with her coat. She said, 'Thank you for inviting me here. I've enjoyed it.'

'Now tell me the truth.'

She faced him earnestly. 'Oh, but I have, I really have.'

'Thanks,' he replied, without expression.

He took her home. On the way she offered, 'If you want any help with moving, let me know, won't you?'

He asked, concentrating on avoiding with his eyes the oncoming lights of other cars, 'What sort of help?'

'Well, packing up your things, books and so on.'

He said, without taking his eyes off the road, 'Thanks, I may take you up on that.'

He drew up outside her house. 'Will you come in?' she asked, expecting him to refuse.

'All right.'

'I don't suppose Roland's back yet.' He got out of the car. 'And Dad's probably up in his room.' He followed her to the front door and into the hall. They stood looking at each other and she did not know how to deal with him.

'Come into the sitting-room,' she invited at last, hoping he would say he had to go. But he accepted. She sat in an armchair, expecting him to do the same, but he stood in front of her, took her hand and hauled her up to face him.

There was an odd anticipation in his eyes that worried her.

'Shall we initiate her into the mysteries of the goodnight kiss?' She drew away as far as his hold would allow.

'No, thank you.'

'Bearing in mind the fact that she's going to get a boy-friend any day now——'

'No, I'm not.'

'I think,' he went on relentlessly, 'it's time she had a little instruction.' He pulled her towards him and she began to resist. It did not deter him, he merely pulled harder. One arm went round her waist and the other to the back of her head, pressing against her hair and propelling her mouth towards his. His lips closed on hers in a cool, gentle kiss.

The kiss went on, still gentle, still tender, and she realised she had stopped resisting and was yielding more and more until almost imperceptibly the pressure of his mouth increased and his hold on her body moved and tightened.

It came to her through the mists of ecstasy that the nature of his kiss was changing and he was demanding from her a response which, if she gave it, would reveal her

93

cherished secret, her love for him. And that was something she had to keep from him at all costs. He must never guess her secret as long as he lived.

She took her hands from his back and put them against his chest, pushing with all her strength, at the same time twisting and turning and prising her mouth from his.

'What are you trying to do,' she choked, backing away, 'testing my morals, like Mrs. Carter, seeing how far I'll let you go without a ring on my finger?'

He moved to stand in front of her, his face pale, his breathing deep but controlled. 'I may be a man without a woman,' he said, 'but by heaven, even I would not waste my time trying to get a response from a piece of marble. And that, my *friend*, is about as much effect as you have on me. Look at my hand,' he held it out, 'not a tremor. Feel my pulse—as steady and regular and unhurried as the tick of a clock.'

She put her hands to her ears. 'You're not only insulting,' she cried, 'you're cruel. You're telling me, *telling* me—to my face—just how ineffective I am in arousing a man's feelings, what a dead loss I am as a woman.' Her voice broke. 'As if I didn't know, *as if I didn't know*!' She turned away, moved her hands to her face and started to cry.

He did not move. He said, at last, 'Let's face it, Elise, we just don't get on, do we? We're like chalk and cheese, water and oil. We just don't mix. You dislike me so much you can't see me as I really am, like seeing my image reflected all the time in a distorting mirror. And my feelings for you——' he shrugged as if they were too trivial to put into words.

'They're non-existent,' she mumbled, 'go on, say it. I can take it.'

'Thanks,' he said crisply, 'for supplying the word I was looking for.' There was a moment's silence then, 'Good-night, Elise.' He let himself out of the house.

Some time later, Roland came in. He found her huddled in the armchair, her eyes heavy and staring, her hand to her head. But he didn't even notice. She lifted her lids and looked at him.

He was euphoric. He flung himself on the couch. 'Hallo,' he said, 'had a good evening?'

She nodded. 'You?'

'Marvellous.' He stared into the distance and drifted back in time. 'Wonderful girl. I want to marry her, Elise.'

His sister sat up. 'You *what*?'

'I'm going to marry her.'

'Does she—does she know?'

'Not yet. I'll tell her soon.'

She put her hands to her cheeks. Events were moving so fast she could not keep up with them. 'How do you know she'll accept?'

'She will.'

This was her brother talking, it was not a dream. He really was sitting there, his head resting on the back of the couch, a reminiscent smile on his face, his eyes bright with love for a girl he had only met the day before.

Envy turned her sour and she chided herself even as she spoke, knowing that although her words had not a grain of truth in them, they would dim his happiness and corrode it with anxiety.

'Don't leave it too long, will you? Your friend Lester's on the prowl, looking for a girl-friend.' She dragged herself out of the chair. 'So be warned. You know what they say about love and war.'

She saw him frown, saw the light in his eyes go out. 'Lester wouldn't do a thing like that.' He looked at her appealingly. 'Would he?'

She went out of the room, saying, 'I wouldn't trust him an inch.'

She climbed the stairs, hating herself, wishing she could

95

take back every word. She heard him mutter to himself, 'Tomorrow. I'll ask her tomorrow.'

'I heard you had a date last night,' Clare remarked as Elise arrived next morning. 'With the great Lester Kings.'

'It wasn't really a date. I listened to his new stereo equipment.'

'Oh.' The silence that followed was like a question mark.

Elise hung her coat in the cupboard and asked, 'Did you enjoy your outing with my brother?'

'It was—very enjoyable, thanks. We talked a lot. It was fun.'

Elise glanced at her, wondering at her guarded reply. Then it occurred to her that they were both playing the same game—trying to hide the truth, but judging by Clare's expression, her secret was obviously a much happier one than her own.

'I'm seeing him again tonight,' Clare said, and she sounded almost guilty.

Elise went up to her. 'Clare,' she said shyly, 'I'm glad, really glad.' And they hugged each other. 'It's wonderful for me as well as Roland.'

They laughed and chatted for a few minutes. 'But I wish,' said Clare, 'you didn't look so miserable. Are you well?'

'Perfectly, thanks. Don't worry about me. Just go on being happy, then perhaps some of it will rub off on me!'

Elise was on her way home at lunchtime when she decided to brave Lester's anger and visit Dawes Hall woods —she corrected herself ruefully—it was Dawes Hall estate these days. Now that the felling contractors had done their worst and vanished from the site, why should she stay away? Lester could not keep her out.

After lunch, she dressed in slacks, sweater and jacket, pulled on her boots and set off on the familiar walk. She flinched a little from the thought of the changes that would greet her. She tried resolutely to banish from her mind the image of the woods as they used to be.

She crossed the railway bridge, pressed on up the hill, along the road that was once bordered by towering elms. Most of them had gone and so had the ruined house. Where the entrance to the woods used to be stood a white board. Painted on it in large black letters were the word 'Kings, Builders' and below it was the familiar slogan, *'Live like Kings in a Monarch House.'* Above the word 'Monarch' were two small crowns, the Kings' trade mark. Beside the board was a Kings' van, empty.

Where the path through the trees used to be was a road. Where the trees used to stand were concrete foundations of houses to be built. Instead of the shrubs and blackberry bushes there were piles of earth and bricks, timber stacked high, discarded sections of drainpipes and bags of cement powder carefully covered with tarpaulins to keep them dry.

A dump truck came chugging along the road and Elise had to step aside to allow it to pass. The driver, wearing a yellow safety helmet with two 'Monarch' crowns on the front, grinned at her and wolf-whistled. A giant-sized excavator threw aside the earth it had shovelled into its scoop. A cement-mixer tossed its contents about with noisy abandon.

A few trees had been spared, as Lester had said, a cypress, an elm and a beech or two. There were huts everywhere. One of them marked 'Site Agent and Clerk of Works' was, she supposed, Lester's. She decided to take no chances in case he was there, so she hurried past, only to stop, shocked into momentary panic by the sound of his voice.

He was standing a short distance away talking to a man who was studying a large sheet of paper—probably the plans of a house—and Lester was running his forefinger over them, pointing something out. He was so absorbed in his discussion he could not possibly have seen her.

She thought it prudent to get herself out of sight until he had gone, so she stepped off the road, picked her way across the builders' rubble and made for the shelter of a half-built brick wall. Balancing one foot in front of the other, she walked along a duckboard spanning a large hole and stepped down alongside the wall.

It was then that she saw the man, half sitting, half lying against the brickwork he was supposed to be working on. He was smoking and it looked as if he was taking an unofficial break. He saw her and stood up, taking his time about it. The look in his eyes should have warned her, but fear fixed her feet securely to the spot. With his heel he ground out the cigarette he had been smoking. He was short, his black hair smoothed down with grease, the state of his face suggesting that he had not shaved for some days.

He swaggered towards her, head slightly down, a gloating look in his sharp eyes. 'Hallo, sweetheart. Come for a chat?'

She took a short agitated step backwards and with it just cleared the end of the half-built wall. She turned to walk over the plank again, saw the hole beneath it, hesitated, and as she did so, his hand closed on her arm. She made a vain effort to wrench it away.

'Stop it!' she said, trying to shout but croaking instead. Then a little louder, 'Stop it!'

She looked round wildly for help, but the man jerked her back behind the shelter of the wall. Footsteps came running along the road, there was a shout, the sound of rubble being disturbed by heavy-booted feet and a voice ordered, 'Take your hands off that girl, Wayman!' The man dropped her arm at once.

'Now you, Elise.' Lester motioned with his head. 'Get out.'

But Elise could not move. Her legs would not function, her feet would not obey.

Lester snapped, 'You're fired, Wayman.'

98

'Now look, boss,' the man whined, 'no harm done. I wasn't going to do anything to her...'

But Lester said, walking away, 'Come to the site office and get your cards.'

'Have a heart, boss,' Wayman moved to stand in front of him, 'don't be so hard. I've got a wife...'

'You should have thought of her before you put your hands on that girl.'

'But, Lester,' Elise said, and he swung round towards her, 'I'm perfectly all right——'

'You keep out of this.' Then to the man, 'Come on, Wayman. Two weeks' pay in lieu of notice. And that's more than some firms would give you in the circumstances.'

Elise saw the ugly look that passed across the man's face and recoiled as if she had been physically assaulted. But Lester had walked on and missed it. She followed at a distance, intending to slip away unnoticed, although Lester, it seemed, had other ideas.

'I want to see you, Elise,' he said, unlocking the site office door and letting himself in.

'I'm going home, Lester.'

He repeated icily, 'I want to see you, Elise.'

She shrugged and rested her shoulders sulkily against the side of the hut. The man was not kept long in the site office, and when he came out he leered at her. 'Thanks for sticking up for me, girlie. Pity we were interrupted, but better luck next time, eh?' He waved insultingly and went off.

Lester called her in. She stood in the doorway, sullen and resentful, hands thrust into her jacket pockets.

'Close the door,' he said. She obeyed him, with her foot.

His arm was resting on the top of a filing cabinet and he was twisting a pencil between his fingers. 'Now. Tell me why you came, when I distinctly told you to stay away from this site.'

She muttered, 'Just looking round.' Then she rallied, resenting his questioning. 'Why shouldn't I come here? I used to walk through the woods almost every day before you and your grandfather murdered them. Where else can I go?'

'You can go where the hell you like,' he countered angrily, 'except to this building site. It's private property, owned by my grandfather and myself.'

'But you can't expect to keep the general public off building sites. They have to come to inspect the houses before deciding to buy.'

'Quite right, but people like that come on legitimate business. You aren't the "general public". When you come here, you're trespassing. And you're a distraction. The men I've got working for me at the moment are a nice enough lot, but they're only human. When I take men on, I don't go into their backgrounds or their pasts, only their work potential. We can't avoid getting one or two doubtful ones, as you've discovered by experience. We just have to take our chance.' He tapped the pencil on the palm of his hand and his smile became insulting. 'Of course, I've heard of women who haunt building sites like "camp followers", but I didn't think you were one of them, although——' his eyes flickered suggestively over her, 'I could be wrong.'

His taunt went home and she coloured deeply. She took a few moments to recover, then said, 'According to you, I have no effect whatsoever on a man, so why worry about my powers of distraction?' He said nothing, merely continued tapping the pencil. The movement began to irritate her and she blurted out bitterly, 'Of course, I forgot, it wasn't men in general, was it? It was you in particular I had no effect on.'

He dropped the pencil but made no attempt to pick it up. He changed his position to lean back with both his elbows on top of the filing cabinet and considered her as attentively as if he were studying the plans of a house.

She went on, 'That's something you excel at, insulting me,' she pushed the pencil round the floor with her foot, 'with your own special brand of abuse. I ought to be used to it by now, but——' She looked up quickly, hoping he had not noticed. He had.

'So my insults upset you, do they?' he drawled. 'Now that surprises me. If you hate me as much as you say you do, they ought to pass over your head.'

She was silent, afraid of giving herself away again. Then she kicked the pencil to the other side of the hut and went to the door.

'I take it you've got the message?' he asked mildly.

'Message or no message,' she snapped, ignoring the anger building up in his eyes, 'you're not keeping me off this site.'

'There are ways,' he said nastily, 'of keeping intruders off building sites—by the use of guard dogs. So if I'm pushed too far, you'll know what to expect. And I'd hate to have to extricate you from the jaws of one of those animals. Just pass that message round your confederates and fellow protesters, will you? It might save an awful lot of trouble.'

She frowned, not believing him. 'You wouldn't do that. Those dogs are vicious creatures. There would be protests.'

She saw his slow, derisive smile and knew how foolish she had been to think that the threat of demonstrations would make any difference to him. He would deal with those as he had dealt with the others—with contempt.

She went out, slamming the door so hard the hut shook under the impact.

CHAPTER VII

ELISE decided not to ask her brother how his friendship with Clare was progressing. She did not relish the rebuff that would have come her way if she had. Nor did she mention it to Clare. But judging by her colleague's bright eyes and the aura of contentment which surrounded her, Elise guessed that all was well.

While part of her resented the fact that her friendship with Clare had been brought to such an abrupt end, the more charitable side of her nature delighted in the fact that her brother, after years of undiluted bachelorhood, had so easily and with such certainty found the woman with whom he wished to share the rest of his life.

Harold Lennan appeared to be taking in his stride his son's acquisition of a girl-friend. It did not seem to worry him that one day Roland might want to set up a home of his own. He had said often enough that if ever his children decided to leave him, he would not stand in their way, and that he would be quite capable of looking after himself.

Elise was alone, as usual, one evening when the telephone rang. With a flick of excitement she recognised the voice.

'Lester here. I'm moving tomorrow from my digs. Could you oblige as promised and help me pack?'

'Of course, Lester. When, afternoon or evening?'

'Both, probably. Is that too much? You could have some food here if necessary.' She agreed. 'Good.' He added cynically, 'If it does nothing else, it will give the landlady something to talk about to her friends and neighbours.' He rang off.

She made her own way to Lester's digs. She had dressed for the part, putting on her old black slacks and a sleeveless cotton top. The landlady let her in, eyebrows exaggeratedly raised. 'Mr. Kings is out, dear.'

'Yes, I know, but he won't be long. I've come to help him pack.'

'*Have* you, dear?' The inflection was nicely calculated to imply the faintest breath of scandal, and Elise responded to the implication too quickly, chiding herself afterwards.

'He said he needed help and we're old friends, you see . . .'

'*Are* you, dear?' The insinuation was there again, but

102

this time Elise was not drawn. She ran up the stairs, eager to get away from those probing eyes which, judging by the minute examination they were making of her clothes, were memorising every detail to pass on to interested neighbours.

Chaos greeted her. Lester had made some attempt to gather his things together, but there had obviously been no method in his efforts. There were two packing cases in the living-room and one in the bedroom. His possessions appeared to have been thrown into them, with no regard for order or preservation of the contents. He did not seem to know that the more neatly things were packed, the more the containers would hold.

Elise took out one by one the items he had hopefully put into the packing cases and painstakingly repacked them, leaving much more room than before. She wrapped break-able ornaments in soft clothes and tucked books into empty corners.

By the time Lester turned the key in the lock and came sprinting up the stairs, she had packed two large suitcases with clothes and filled cartons and boxes with books and other personal belongings.

He paused in the doorway, taking in at a glance the pro-gress she had made. 'You must have worked damned hard to achieve this,' was his comment as he crossed the room to her side. 'You really did mean it when you said you'd help, didn't you? Some women I know would have sat around until I arrived and then roused themselves to put the kettle on and make some tea, while I got down to it!'

She flushed at his compliment and smiled up at him. 'You obviously don't know the right women.'

'You're dead right. I'll have to go out of my way to cultivate this one, won't I?' His arm rested lightly round her waist, but she moved quickly out of range.

'There's still plenty for you to do, though. You've got so many books! There are those two shelves by the fireplace to clear. Could you get on with it?'

'Are you giving me orders in my own territory, young woman?'

'Yes.' She smiled. 'I'm organising you. It's about time someone took you in hand.' He approached her menacingly, but she backed away. 'The chaos that greeted me when I arrived nearly made me turn and run.'

As his hand reached out to get her, she did turn and run—into the bedroom. She attempted to clear the dressing-table, but it was in such a state of disorder, being strewn with documents and papers connected with his work, she decided it might be more prudent to let Lester tackle it himself. As she turned to call him, her eye was caught by the glint of glass amongst the layers of paper. It looked like a photograph. She extricated it carefully and found that it was. Across a corner was a message written in a neat, feminine hand. 'To Lester,' it said, 'with my everlasting love, Nina.'

As Elise studied the beautiful face, the regular features, the perfect nose and mouth, eyes which were innocent yet challenging, her heart sank. She thought miserably, 'No wonder he was heartbroken at losing her. A girl like that would only have to lift her finger and any man, even Lester, would go running back at her command.'

'Yes,' said a voice at the door, 'I thought it wouldn't be long before you found that.' He stood at her side. 'She's pretty, isn't she, my ex-fiancée? The only thing she lacked was constancy.' His eyes laughed at her in the dressing-table mirror. 'But women are faithless creatures, aren't they? And I don't suppose you're an exception. Are you?'

She ignored his question and put down the photograph, bending over the papers and trying to get them into some sort of order.

'You haven't answered me, Elise.' She looked up, surprised by his change of tone, as though he really expected an answer.

She tried to supply one. 'Well, I—I don't——'

'No, of course you don't know. You've never been given the chance to find out.' He was being cynical again and this, oddly, she found easier to cope with than his sudden sincerity. 'Your constancy has never been tested by any man yet, has it? According to Roland, you've never had a real boy-friend. I find that astonishing.'

He threw himself full-length on the bed and pulled her down to sit beside him. 'Aren't you afraid of being alone in a bedroom with a philandering, libidinous bachelor, who has publicly renounced women except for what he can get out of them? Or are you really so incredibly innocent that you're quite unaware of the dangers implicit in such a situation?'

She smiled uncertainly, not knowing how to take him. Looking at him lying there, she thought he was quite capable of getting whatever he wanted from a woman. And, there was no doubt about it, she was fully aware of the dangers—the tantalisingly attractive dangers—of being alone with him in such a situation.

But her one protection from him—and from herself—was her cloak of innocence and this she flung hastily round her. She nodded.

He smiled incredulously. 'Are you being serious?' She felt a gentle tug as he started to impel her down towards him. 'You tempt me,' he murmured, 'to give you a practical demonstration of the hazards involved. After all, who better than an old—and shall we say trusted—friend of the family to introduce you to the salacious pleasures of the flesh?' His eyes wandered appreciatively over her. 'There's no doubt about it,' he said softly, 'you need something, some catalyst to turn you into a living, breathing woman, instead of just an extension of a piece of radio equipment.'

His mockery stung her. She jerked her hand away and pulled herself upright. Like the young Lester tormenting her on the swing, the mature Lester was tormenting her now.

105

'I came to help with the packing,' she said acidly, 'not for a lesson in seduction. Anyway, we act as abrasives on each other, don't we? Like chalk and cheese, you said—we just don't mix.' She carried on with the work.

He lay there for some time watching her and when she could not stand it any longer, she went out of the room. He soon joined her and they worked in silence side by side.

The landlady brought them some food which they ate while they packed. When the work was finished, he took her home. As she opened the car door, he thanked her.

'I'm more than grateful, and I mean that.' His hand came out to prevent her from getting out of the car. 'Tell me something. Why did you do it? Was there a motive, a reason? I'd honestly like to know.'

'Of course there wasn't a motive. I did it because you needed help, that's all. And perhaps for old times' sake. After all,' she got out and stood on the pavement, 'we used to be friends, didn't we?'

He phoned a few days later and she asked him, 'Did your moving pass off without a hitch?'

'Yes, mainly thanks to your excellent packing. Mrs. Dennis took over at the other end. She "organised" me, as you would put it. She also praised your handiwork. Er—changing the subject, you remember I mentioned a chap called Howard Beale?'

'Yes,' she answered, moistening her lips, 'why?'

'He'd like to meet you. Can I bring him round?'

'But, Lester, I didn't think you meant it. You know very well I don't want——'

'He's standing beside me, Elise.' His voice was warning her to be more guarded. 'We'll be round in ten minutes.'

He cut off and Elise was left staring stupidly at the receiver. She replaced it slowly and looked down at the clothes she was wearing—old black trousers, black too-tight sweater. She shrugged. What of it? She didn't aim to impress the man. If her appearance put him off, all the better.

She tidied the sitting-room, plumping up the cushions and picking up the magazines and newspapers strewn over the floor, then ran upstairs. They arrived before the ten minutes were up. She heard the doorbell ring and her father answered it. She combed her hair and fluffed a layer of powder over her face.

They were in the hall when she went down. Lester watched her, his face a study in blankness. Then she saw the man he had brought with him.

He was of medium height, as solid in build as apparently in bank balance, prosperity and success sitting smugly on his shoulders and giving him an air of pomposity and of premature age. He could not have been much more than thirty-five, but he looked like a man whose mental outlook was of someone approaching retirement.

He stared boldly at Elise as she stood quietly at Lester's side, waiting for him to introduce them. She knew at once she would not like him. Even if her heart had not been given in its entirety to Lester Kings, she would not have spared this stolid, dull-looking person another thought.

But Howard Beale looked like a man who had just been offered a good bargain at a surprisingly reasonable price. He seemed satisfied with the girl Lester Kings was presenting to him as a prospective wife.

They shook hands and moved into the sitting-room, but Elise did not alter her expression. She kept it apathetic and blank, and as they sat down, Howard in the armchair, Lester beside her on the couch, she made no attempt to converse.

Howard tried talking to her, but she gave monosyllabic answers. The more irritated Lester became, the more she played the dull-witted, slow-thinking, untutored girl. Once, when Howard was searching in his pockets for a cigarette, which he had first asked permission to smoke, she glanced at Lester and caught the impact of his wrath. She flashed him a sudden, intentionally impish grin, then allowed her surliness to close down again.

Lester moved his two hands together in a throttling action as though he would dearly have loved to put her neck between them. It was a lightning communication which could only have taken place between old friends who knew each other intimately, or lovers. The unspoken message was understood instantly by both. But Elise chose to ignore it.

'Would you like a cup of tea?' she asked, speaking her first complete sentence.

Lester looked at Howard, who accepted eagerly, probably, Elise thought, to rid himself of her impossibly stupid presence for a few minutes. She made the tea and carried it in on a tray.

'I'll take a cup to your father,' Lester said, standing in front of her and grinning triumphantly. She frowned, uncertain now. His move had put her in check, and he knew it. With Lester upstairs talking to her father, she would be forced to make reasonably sensible conversation with the other man, with no intermediary to protect her.

As soon as Lester had gone, Howard moved to sit beside her. He accepted a cup of tea and took out his diary.

'Since we've got to get to know each other,' he said, and Elise was astonished that his skin was so thick he could take her lack of response as encouragement, 'we must decide on a date to meet.'

She floundered. 'Oh, I—I don't think, I mean I don't know whether——' She might have saved her breath. He went on blandly,

'The evenings are getting longer, so a drive is called for I think, then we can discuss the position.'

'For heaven's sake,' she thought, 'what position?'

'Couldn't we——?' she said aloud, hesitated, decided to be more positive, and went on, 'Could we go to a concert?'

He shook his head. 'Not my cup of tea at all. I'm tone deaf. I find it agony listening to music.'

Lester came back, a half-smile on his face betraying that he had heard Howard's dismissal of what was so dear to her. 'Now a show, a good show—plenty of colour, dancing, movement. Not to mention the girls that go with it.' He threw a sly smile at Lester. 'Now that I do like. Tell you what I'll do, I'll look in the paper and see what's on, and give you a ring.'

Elise said faintly, helpless in the face of his unbelievable insensibility, 'If you like,' at the same time experiencing a sense of reprieve at even so small a delay in the continuance of their acquaintance.

He nodded smugly. She felt that even if she had said 'no, thank you' his reaction would have been the same, because it would not have filtered through his complacency and conceit that she could possibly have refused.

Soon afterwards, Lester suggested it was time to go. He lingered in the hall after Howard had gone out to the car.

'Did you have to play the complete dimwit?' he whispered, like a conspirator.

'I didn't ask you to bring him,' she snapped. 'If you will act like a self-appointed marriage bureau, don't blame me if your manoeuvres have misfired and I don't approve of your choice of marriage partner for me.'

Howard wound down the window of Lester's car and cleared his throat noisily. Lester took the hint.

'Anyway,' Elise called softly as he moved away down the path, 'I told you, I don't want to get married,' adding childishly, 'and what's more, you can't make me!'

The impatient backward movement of his hand was both a dismissal and a terse reminder that Howard might be listening and she should therefore have had more tact.

The next afternoon Phil Pollard answered the phone and looked suspicious when he handed the receiver to Elise.

'It's a man asking for you,' he said frowning, then more hopefully, 'it could be your brother.'

She shook her head, and dreaded hearing the caller's

109

voice. 'Elise Lennan here,' she said almost inaudibly.

'How can I be sure,' said the voice which set her heart pounding, 'that it's not a mouse I'm talking to?'

She laughed and relief put unusual warmth into her answer. 'Oh, Lester,' she said, 'it's you.'

Phil's head shot round, his eyes full of mistrust. She turned away hoping a little childishly that such an action might prevent him from hearing the conversation.

'Are you so glad to hear from me,' Lester said, 'that you come alive at the sound of my voice?' She could hear that he was smiling. 'I'm touched—and flattered—by your sudden change of heart towards me.'

'It's not that,' she said hurriedly, 'I thought it might be——'

'Don't spoil this sudden rapport between us. It's so rare I feel I want to cherish this moment for ever.'

'Stop being silly, Lester.' She glanced apprehensively at Phil, who was beginning to look annoyed. 'What do you want?'

'What's the matter?' Lester asked, lowering his voice. 'Is your boss getting jealous? I must make a habit of phoning you at work, or better still, call in. That would really get him worried. He'd think I was after you.'

'I'm perfectly well aware,' she mouthed into the receiver, 'that even if I were the last woman on earth, you wouldn't be "after me". Now will you tell me what you want?'

He was laughing so loudly she had to hold the receiver away from her ear. When he had recovered he said, 'The little mouse shows some spirit after all. Maybe I misjudged her?'

'Goodbye, Lester,' she said, and prepared to ring off.

'Wait a minute,' he urged, 'at least let me give you my message. It's from my grandfather. His secretary has gone off to help her daughter cope with her new-born infant, as expected. Could you oblige as promised?'

'When—tomorrow?'

'This afternoon if possible.' She hesitated and he said softly, 'Could you—please?'

She said 'All right' with a sigh and asked how would she get there?

'I won't be free in time to take you so could you go by bus? I'll take you home afterwards.'

She agreed and rang off. She saw the query in Phil's eyes and knew she would have to explain. He did not like what he heard.

'You don't mean you're actually going to help old man Kings? I thought you were as much against them and their damnable desecration of the countryside as I am. Or,' with a guardedly jealous look, 'has that grandson of his persuaded you to go over to their side?'

'Of course not, Mr. Pollard.' But despite her emphatic denial of collusion, she felt a twinge of conscience as she saw the hurt in his eyes.

There was the smell of floor polish, liberally and energetically applied as the housekeeper opened the door of Alfred Kings' residence.

'Mrs. Dennis?' Elise asked as she stepped into the hall.

'I am, my dear,' said the housekeeper, smiling and bustling in front of her across the shining parquet floor. 'And you're Elise Lennan. We've been told to expect you. I remember you, dear, when you were a little girl.' She turned, her hand on the door handle. 'You and Mr. Lester and your brother used to go roaming in those woods, didn't you, climbing trees and getting your clothing torn?' She waggled her head from side to side, her ample chins following suit a few seconds later. 'And now they've all gone, those trees. I told Mr. Kings he shouldn't have done it.'

Her round motherly shape moved busily into the lounge. With its fitted carpeting, its wall-lights, the delicate decor and luxurious furniture, it was a room that spelt comfort and opulence and an unmistakable desire to impress. It was in essence a perfect example of late twentieth-century taste.

Only the occupant struck a false note. He might have come from Edwardian times, with his stiff high collar, the waistcoat buttoned beneath his jacket and the pocket watch with its heavy gold chain. The man himself was lithe and wiry, his eyes alert with a kind of cunning, his hair white and sparse. He wore his years with unbelievable ease and his wits seemed to be as lively as those of a man half his age.

When Mrs. Dennis showed Elise into the room, Alfred Kings was sitting, slippered and relaxed on the couch. A cigarette, which, by the stubs in the ash-tray had been preceded by many more, drooped from his puckered lips, and its smell caught at Elise's throat. A glass of beer balanced precariously on the upholstered arm. His hands, with their gnarled knuckles and veins made prominent by age and sheer hard work in days gone by, held up in front of him the morning's newspaper.

He looked like a man who would have been more at home in a Victorian kitchen, but who was determined to live up to the affluent image which he felt was expected of a successful and wealthy builder.

Realising he had a guest, he put the paper down and motioned to Elise with exaggerated gestures to come in and make herself at home.

'You're very welcome, my dear,' he said. 'Cup of tea, or a glass of something?' The wink he gave her advised her to accept the latter. 'Do you good, eh?'

Elise smiled and refused as politely as she could. She wished she could tell him she had come to work, not to be entertained. She wanted to get the preliminaries and polite conversation over as fast as possible.

Mrs. Dennis left them and Elise sank into the cushions of the deeply comfortable armchair. Alfred replenished his glass from the bottle on the table, toasted her and drank, smacking his lips afterwards and admiring the rim round the empty glass.

'Shouldn't have this stuff,' he chuckled. 'Doctor says I mustn't, old mother Dennis says I mustn't, but let them try to stop me, that's all.'

That, Elise thought, was what he had probably said when told of the protests about his intention to cut down Dawes Hall woods. He seemed the sort of man who thrived on opposition, who took resistance as a challenge and who regarded every obstacle put in his way as yet another barrier to be overcome—a characteristic which his grandson seemed to have inherited in abundance.

Alfred leaned back, crossed his short legs and moved a slippered foot up and down, as if even in the act of relaxing, his energy and agility would not entirely let him be.

'So my grandson's got round you, has he, to come and help us out? Got a way with him, that boy, got a way with women, just like his old grandfather at his age!' He chuckled. 'Only I was a married man with a handful of kids!'

He grinned at her meaningfully as if trying to get across the implication behind his words. She smiled politely, remembering what his grandson had said about his admiration of a man with a long list of girl-friends.

He sighed, as if nostalgic for the old days. 'Now I let my grandson get on with it. Fit as I feel, I'm past seventy-seven, and that's no age to be running a business, however much money it might be putting into your pocket.' He put his glass on the carpet at his feet and promptly knocked it over. It rolled unheeded under the couch.

Furtively Elise glanced at her watch. Time was passing and she wished she could think of a polite way of telling him so.

'Ah,' he said, 'things were different in the old days. An employer got the most he could out of his workers. Nothing namby-pamby about the building trade then.' He settled more comfortably into the upholstery. 'Did you know, girl,

113

that if a man was five minutes late for work, he'd lose fifteen minutes' pay? If it was wet, he'd still be expected to work, or he'd lose money. Now,' he commented disgustedly, 'they coddle 'em. My grandson, for instance, he's the same, too easygoing by half, I tell him.'

'My grandfather has a captive audience, I see.'

Elise started violently at the sound of Lester's voice, but Alfred Kings did not move a muscle. He did not even turn his head.

Lester stood in the doorway, a smile softening the cynical twist to his mouth. He was in working clothes, mud-stained here and there. He lounged against the doorway, looking from one to the other.

'Come in, lad,' his grandfather invited.

'If I trod the sacred pile of that carpet in these boots,' Lester answered dryly, 'I'd have Mrs. Dennis on to me like the proverbial ton of bricks.'

His grandfather hooted, 'And that, boy, would be an experience you'd never forget!'

Lester asked Elise, raising his eyebrows, 'I take it you haven't done a stroke of work?'

She flushed at the suggestion that she was slacking.

'Work?' the old man said with a jerky laugh, 'You young 'uns don't know what work is. D'you know, my dear,' and Lester raised his eyes skywards as if to say 'he's off again', 'they treat the workmen these days like they was royalty. They don't have to make their own way to work now, they're taken out in the firm's buses to the sites they're working on, and what's more,' he waggled his finger, 'they pay them from the time of getting on the bus, not just from the time they arrive at the site, like it used to be. Now they pay men for holidays—that's something they never did when I was a lad. *And* they get a winter holiday as well as a summer one!'

'Elise has come to work, Grandfather,' Lester reminded him gently, but he might as well have stayed silent for all

114

the effect it had on his grandfather's locquaciousness.

'And I'll tell you something else, girl. All this talk of "day release" at the local tech. In the good old days, the lads had to do it in their own time, in the evenings, when they was dead tired after a day's work. Now they get jam on it—it's in the terms of apprenticeship, it's compulsory, they all get it—in the day, and have to take time off work. *And* they don't lose any pay.' He shook his head and did not notice Lester beckoning Elise from the room.

He went on talking to himself as she went out, 'In those days, a builder paid for what he got and got what he paid for. Now . . .'

His voice faded away as Lester indicated that Elise should follow him along the hall. The study opened out of the morning room, and Lester told her they used both rooms for the administrative side of the business.

'These are our offices—as you can see from the chaos all around you!'

The table was laden with folders and plans, the chairs piled high with papers. Even the floor had not escaped. It was strewn with opened letters and discarded envelopes and magazines concerned with the building trade.

'This is my office,' they went into the study, 'but as I'm here so rarely, we've put the typist's desk in here, too.' He smiled at her. 'Don't look so worried. I told you, I'm not often in residence, so you won't be burdened too often with my presence.'

She asked uncertainly, 'Who will give me work? Your grandfather or——?'

He said softly, his smile mocking, 'I shall be giving you work, not my grandfather.'

'But,' she said, her eyes accusing him of misrepresentation, 'you told me it was your grandfather who needed help.'

'And if I had told you it was I who needed it, you would have run a mile, wouldn't you?'

'So you got me here under false pretences?'

He moved away so that his face was turned from her. 'I got you here because the firm,' he emphasised the word, 'needed help, and out of the kindness of your heart, you agreed to come. I think that's a good enough explanation of my request. Now,' he said, his eyes narrowing a little, 'can we put aside our habitual enmity and forget our personal differences and get on?'

She apologised, removed her jacket and sat down at the typewriter.

'It's an old tank,' he remarked, tapping two or three keys with his forefinger, 'but it works—just.'

She opened a drawer and found a pencil and note-pad. 'Will I need these?'

He was sitting on the edge of her desk, facing her, and reading through a batch of letters. 'What? Yes, you'll need those. I'll dictate answers to these letters.'

For the next half-hour she took shorthand notes. He spoke so fluently and so fast, she found to her chagrin she was lagging behind and was forced to ask him to repeat much of what he had said. He would smile in a superior fashion and deliberately speak slowly and over-clearly for a few minutes, then speed up again.

At the end he turned, 'If you had me as a boss permanently, I'd make you go to refresher classes to brush up your shorthand speed.'

He watched her eyes cloud over with something like pain and sat swinging his booted leg, waiting for her reaction.

She flung down her pencil like an ill-humoured child and started to rise from the chair. 'If I'm not good enough for you ...'

He leaned forward and caught her shoulders, pushing her down. 'I assure you, my *sweet* Elise, you're quite good enough for me.'

She flushed and frowned, suspecting his words of having a double meaning, but his face gave nothing away.

'Is that all?'

'For the time being, yes.' He moved across the room to sit at his desk.

All the time she was typing, he stayed in the room. When she had finished she asked if he would read them through. He came across to her and rested against the desk, picking up the letters and reading them one by one.

He looked down at her face, flushed with effort, and smiled. 'Very creditable performance. Beautifully presented, not a single mistake. Full marks.'

His praise brought a glow to her features which she could not hide. He leaned forward and caught her chin, forcing her to look at him. 'My word, when you look like that,' he said softly, 'you're irresistible.'

Their eyes met, the room faded and time itself stood still. She moistened her lips and found her voice.

'Even to you?' she whispered.

'Even to me,' he whispered back.

With an effort their eyes disentangled and he returned to his desk. She sat, twisting her hands, her back to him.

'Is that all?' she asked at last.

'That's all, thanks.' He sounded terse. 'If you can hang on for a few minutes, I'll take you home.'

'It doesn't matter. I can get a bus.'

He stood at his desk, reading a letter, and ignored her remark. She put on her jacket and sat down again.

He dropped the letter. 'Ready?' he asked.

They went out the back way. 'I haven't said goodbye to your grandfather.'

'I assure you, he won't even notice.'

She wondered why he sounded so short-tempered. 'I'm afraid it'll have to be the van. My car's being serviced.'

She opened the passenger's door, picked up the white safety helmet which she assumed was Lester's, and settled uncomfortably into the hard seat. As he joined the traffic on the main road, she examined the helmet on her lap, noting the two crowns—the Kings' crest—on the front.

'How is it,' she asked, 'that your helmet is white but other men on the site have yellow or red ones?'

'Ah, now, that's a sort of colour coding. People in charge, like me, and visitors, wear white ones. Others, such as drivers, operators of mechanical equipment like excavators and so on, wear yellow. Bricklayers and the like wear red.'

'So you can see at a glance who is doing what by the colour of their safety helmets?'

'Correct.' He smiled. 'An intelligent deduction, which is what I would have expected from my old friend's sister.'

She coloured at his second compliment of the day. 'Thanks.' She went on, 'Are helmets compulsory?'

'They are, but it's not unusual for some of the men to take them off, although if I catch them doing it, they get a rocket from me.' After a pause he asked, in an odd tone, 'How's friend Pollard these days? Still organising protest meetings about the new estate?'

'I don't think so,' she answered slowly. 'Why?'

He didn't reply. Instead he asked another question. 'Has he accepted the house-building as an inescapable fact of life?'

'I doubt it. He still gets angry when the subject is mentioned.'

'Oh.' He shot her a glance. 'And you? Have you accepted it, or does the sight of those houses going up goad you into a self-righteous fury?'

She frowned, wondering what he was getting at. 'Yes,' she said shortly.

'And yet you still agreed to come and help me, or rather my grandfather, in the office?'

She laughed without humour. 'I see what you mean. Ironic, isn't it?'

'Very,' he commented dryly. 'Unless it was my magnetic charm you couldn't resist?'

It was a question she refused to answer. Instead she

118

asked another. 'When will you want me to help you again?'

'So you're still willing to collaborate with the enemy?' She looked at him quickly, wondering if he was serious, but he was smiling. 'You're a glutton for punishment, aren't you?'

What was he trying to prove—that she was only too ready to go against her principles? She battled with her conscience which was struggling to tell her he was right.

'So you don't want my help?' she snapped, realising too late that her display of irritation would tell him that his taunt had hit the target.

'But of course I do.' His voice was silky soft. 'You're indispensable to me.' His hand covered hers until she snatched it away. His tone returned to normal. 'I'll let you know when. In a day or two probably.'

He pulled up outside her house and she got out. He asked, 'Will Roland be in this evening?'

'I'm sorry, but I don't know my brother's movements these days. Once I could have said "yes" without hesitation, but now——'

'He's unpredictable now he's got a woman in tow?' She didn't answer. 'All right, I'll call in just in case.' She turned away. 'Elise.' She stopped. 'Thanks for your help.'

She smiled briefly over her shoulder and went in.

After the evening meal, her father went up to his room as usual. Elise told Roland, 'Lester said he would come this evening.'

'Oh. That's awkward. Clare's coming.'

She shrugged. 'Then he'll just have to go away again, won't he?'

Clare, she thought bitterly, as she washed up, should be my friend, not Roland's. Lester had called her 'the only friend I've ever had'. Now I've not only lost her, but Roland's companionship too. Once it wouldn't have mattered. Now, her loneliness was a pain she had to learn to endure all over again.

119

Clare came and brought her gaiety with her. Watching Clare with her brother, Elise realised how deeply in love they were. 'It won't be long,' she thought, sitting in the armchair while they held hands on the couch, 'it can't be long before they marry.'

When Lester came, she let him in. He raised his eyebrows and indicated the sitting-room. 'Yes?' he asked.

'Yes, he's in, but Clare's with him.'

'Oh.' He rubbed his chin, hesitating.

'Go in and see them, anyway. I told Roland you were coming.'

He stood at the door, watching them, 'Hallo, you two.'

Roland extended his hand. 'Hallo there. Haven't seen you for some time, Lester.'

'You've been much better occupied, haven't you?' He looked round for a seat and made for the armchair.

Elise beat him to it, and he clenched his fist and playfully pushed it towards her chin. Then he sat on the arm of her chair and smiled at the couple on the couch.

'I must say it's good to see my old friend Roland so happily settled with the lady of his choice.'

'Do you approve?' asked Clare, with a smile.

'Heartily,' came the unequivocal answer. 'Although I myself have renounced women for the rest of my life, I'm nevertheless delighted when I see another man in love with a woman who loves him as deeply as he loves her.'

Elise stirred beside him and he looked down, but her face was resolutely turned away.

'Elise, now,' he said, smiling, 'she's acquired a boy-friend. Has she told you?'

'She hasn't!' Clare was dumbfounded and sat forward out of the circle of Roland's arm. 'What do you mean by keeping this from me, Elise? Who is he? You, Lester?'

He gave a short sardonic laugh. '*Me*? You must be joking! She wouldn't have me as a boy-friend if I were the last man on earth. Would you, Elise?'

She glared at him, knowing he was deliberately playing back to her the words she had used about him.

His arm, which had been resting across the back of her chair, moved down and his fingers lifted her hair and rested against her neck. She jerked away and he removed his hand.

'You see?' he said as if he had just conducted an experiment for his own satisfaction and proved himself to be right, 'she flinches away from my touch, however slight.'

Roland and Clare were studying them with the detached surprise of a devoted couple who, wrapped around by their love, could not believe that everyone else was not in the same ecstatic state.

'Her boy-friend's name,' said Lester, getting up and roaming about the room, 'is Howard Beale. He's a surveyor.'

'This is news, Elise,' said Roland, settling his arm more comfortably round Clare's waist. 'Does Dad know?'

'Of course not. There's nothing to tell. I only met the man last night. Lester introduced us.'

'You like him, don't you, Elise?' She looked up and met Lester's cynical smile. 'Tell them how much you like Howard.'

'*Like* him? How could I like him? He's a pompous ass!'

'But, my dear Elise,' now Lester's smile was goading, 'what does that matter? He's got plenty of money. He could give you everything you could possibly wish for. For instance, the very best in hi-fi equipment...'

'Which he hates.'

'So what? He could even afford to have a room specially sound-proofed so that you could listen to it without disturbing him.'

She rounded on him. 'When—if—I marry, I'll choose someone I can share my likes and dislikes with. Anyway, what are you trying to do—talk me into marrying him? Is that all you think I want,' she cried, fighting the tears that

121

threatened, 'financial security, creature comforts?' Roused to a state of unbearable envy by the sight of the couple on the couch, she jerked herself to her feet. Her voice rose out of control. 'You think all I want to do is to sell myself to the highest bidder?'

She couldn't see his face for tears and she rushed from the room, aware that Roland and Clare were staring open-mouthed at her uncharacteristic display of emotion.

Her bedroom was a refuge and the pillow she pressed against her cheek a solace. She didn't know why she was crying, she only knew that as she did so, she felt an over-whelming relief from the pain inside, the pain of un-returned love.

She quietened at last and lay still, emotionally exhausted. She tensed. Someone was climbing the stairs. It was probably Clare coming to comfort her. The door opened and Lester walked in.

She lifted her head and asked belligerently, 'What do you want?'

He answered quietly, 'To see how you are.'

'I'm not ill. I'm quite all right. You can go.'

He was silent, looking down at her. It was dusk now and the evening sky, flushed with the setting sun, glowed in the west, defying the encroaching clouds bringing darkness.

'Shall I turn on the light?'

'No, thank you.'

'Tell me,' he walked to the window, 'what's wrong with Howard Beale?'

She hesitated. What was the purpose of his question? Was he testing her? 'I—I know I could never love him.' She lifted herself wearily and swung her feet to the floor, smoothing her hair and pressing the back of her hand against a burning cheek. 'And when I marry—*if* I marry—I want love, to give it and receive it, the sort of love my parents shared.'

He turned slowly from the window and leaned back

against the sill. She could not see his face in the darkness. 'Don't fool yourself, Elise. There's no such thing. If a man like Howard Beale—solid as a rock, with a stable, civilised personality—can offer you an assured future free from financial worries, you'd be a fool to refuse him.' He finished bitterly, 'Love? You can have it!'

'How can you say that?' she cried. 'You've only got to look at Roland and Clare to see how wrong you are.'

'They're lucky, luckier than they know. In any case,' he came to sit beside her, hands in pockets, 'I can watch them quite dispassionately, without getting involved. I'm immune now. I just sit on the sidelines and observe others. I don't feel a thing.'

'You're a cynic. You've let yourself turn sour.'

'So what, I've turned sour. At least I won't get hurt any more.'

She despaired. She wished she knew some way of reaching him, of being like other girls who could let a man know they loved him without actually saying so. She forced herself to argue with him because she knew she had to. For the sake of the love she felt for him she had to try to reason him into a less bitter, less jaundiced state of mind.

'And because a girl—one girl—let you down, you've allowed yourself to turn into a heartless, unfeeling——' But he misinterpreted her intention and broke in angrily,

'Here we go again, back to the monotonous recitation of my faults and failings. I know just what you think of me, you've told me often enough, so you can just shut up!'

It was dark now and the only light in the room came from the uncurtained windows of the houses opposite. He stood in silence for some time, staring out. Then he saw the doll lying, passive and lifeless, on the chair. He put his hand round its body and held it up to the window as if examining it. Its outline showed sharply against the semi-darkness beyond the glass. With a shrug, he dropped it back to the chair and went out.

123

NEXT morning Phil Pollard asked her how she felt after her excursion into enemy territory. 'No injuries? No war wounds?'

She smiled. She could not tell him that the only wounds she had received were beneath the surface, invisible and irreparable.

'While you were in Kings' office, did you find out any secrets that might help us in our sabotage attempts?'

By the way he was smiling, she knew he was joking, but his words reminded her uncomfortably of Lester's questions when he had taken her home from the office.

'No,' she laughed, 'I learned nothing which might be of use in that respect. Only things like delivery dates of materials and why certain items hadn't arrived on the days specified and how this was holding up the building schedule.

Clare, who could hear them talking, called from the shop, 'Did you see in the local paper yesterday that Kings are losing a lot of stuff from their site? They suspect someone of stealing it.'

'What sort of stuff?' Phil asked, preoccupied with sharpening a pencil.

Clare appeared at the office door. 'Oh, copper tubing, bags of cement, timber and so on. Even large pieces of scaffolding. The odd thing is, apparently, whoever's doing it knows what he's about because the stuff he's taking is stopping the builders getting on with the job.'

A customer came in and Clare went away to serve her. Elise sat in front of the typewriter. Her eyes were looking through some shorthand notes, but in her thoughts she was back in the Kings' van being questioned by the grandson of the owner. Now she knew what he had been getting at. In a subtle way he had been trying to discover the strength of Phil's feelings about the estate, whether in fact he felt badly enough about it to make him turn thief and try to sabotage the building operations.

'Sabotage'—that was the word Phil had just used. Her heart missed a beat. She looked at his profile. He was unconcernedly looking through a record catalogue. A little too unconcerned, perhaps?

As she began to type, she remembered with a shock that Lester had questioned her about her own feelings too. She stopped typing and felt herself growing hot with humiliation. So he suspected her of theft! Did he perhaps think she was 'collaborating' with Phil? Was his opinion of her as bad as that? She went back to her typing, her fingers pounding the keys, trying desperately to make the clatter drown the answer to the question.

Later that day she got the phone call she had been dreading.

'Howard here,' the caller said. 'I assume you're free this evening, Elise? I've found there's a good play on at the repertory theatre in the town and I've bought a couple of tickets.'

His easy familiarity after only one meeting, his assumption that she was his for the taking and would be willing to follow wherever he led, brought her anger to boiling point. But she reduced the heat until it merely simmered and told him indifferently,

'Yes, I could go with you.'

'Good. I'll call at seven. Goodbye till then.'

He rang off, having made what was obviously to him a business appointment. Before he arrived, she put on her plainest clothes, used to make-up and combed her hair so that it hung, loose and uninterestingly, to her shoulders. She would give him no encouragement either in appearance or behaviour.

But he didn't even notice. He led her to the car, spoke on the way about everyday matters, commented on the pleasant weather they were having and was not put off in

125

the least by her brief replies.

At the theatre they sat in the most expensive seats, shared the most costly box of chocolates the confectionery counter could offer, and in the interval drank the choicest wine in the bar. On the way home they discussed the play, or rather, Howard talked and Elise listened. It was just as well, she thought. She could not have supplied any intelligent remarks with which to punctuate his conversation if he had required any. She hardly knew what the play had been about. She had watched, had, by using her instinct, looked sad and happy at all the right places, but nothing had registered.

He saw her to the front door, leaned forward, caught her shoulders and kissed her briefly on the mouth. He told her they would meet again soon.

As she let herself in, she decided that the kiss had been a premeditated act, part of a plan prepared in advance and decided upon after the situation had been methodically measured and estimated and valued. But as far as she was concerned, the friendship between them was a non-starter. It was over before it had even begun.

Roland called out from his bedroom that Lester had phoned while she was out. Would she go to the office next day and do the work he would leave on the desk?

She put her head round his door. 'Did you tell him I'd gone out with Howard?'

'No. He didn't ask.'

Elise thought that after the things she had said about Howard Beale, it was just as well. She thanked him for taking the message and went to bed.

Mrs. Dennis showed her straight into the office. 'Did you want to see Mr. Kings?' she asked. 'Mr. Lester's not here.'

Elise assured her hastily that it was not necessary to see anyone because the work would be waiting for her.

She removed her cardigan and got down to it. When she

was half-way through, Alfred came wandering in.

'Heard you typing,' he said, moving round the room and shuffling through piles of papers. 'Look at this,' he muttered to himself. 'All these nails he's ordering, and all this paint.' He shook his head. 'I'll have to tell him to cut down. Extravagance, that's what it is.'

His hand, with the merest tremor that revealed his advancing age, felt for the back of Lester's chair, and he slowly lowered himself into it. He started talking and she was forced to stop typing in order to hear what he said.

'In the old days,' he mused, filling a pipe he had taken from his pocket, 'I'd tell the men to go round all the houses we'd finished building, get down on their hands and knees and pick up all the bent nails lying about.' He chuckled. 'Know what I'd do then? I'd tell them to hammer them straight and use 'em again!' He grinned, showing his teeth yellowed with tobacco-smoking. 'Always get the most and give the least, that's always been my motto! And paint, know what I'd do with bits of paint left over? Have 'em all tipped into one tin and stirred together and I'd tell the painters to use it for gutters and such like.' He puffed his pipe into life and Elise recoiled at the unpleasant smell 'Can't do that now, though,' he went on. 'Gutters are made of plastic. *Plastic!*' His disgust was unmistakable.

'And all the regulations you've got to take notice of these days! A builder's bound hand and foot by bits of paper. Now my grandson, he's been brought up in the trade the new way. From the start he's been taught what's right and what's wrong, passed exams and got a string of fancy letters after his name. Me—I had to pick it up the hard way, by learning as I went along.'

Mrs. Dennis called, 'Mr. Kings, cup of tea for you. Ask the young lady if she'd like one, will you?'

But Elise refused politely and watched him go with ill-disguised relief. She opened a window to let out the pipe smell and got down to work again. She had nearly finished

127

when Lester came in. When he heard about his grandfather's remarks, he laughed.

'That's his favourite subject, the old days and the new. He's found the changes hard to accept, which is partly why he got the business into such a muddle and had to call on me to get him out of it.'

'Well,' she said pointing to a paper on the desk, 'this is a change I hadn't heard about, there aren't any local building byelaws any more.'

He came to stand beside her. 'No, there aren't. Building regulations are mandatory now, under an Act of Parliament. So the next time you look over a house which is being built,' he ruffled her hair, 'and don't take that as an open invitation to visit Kings' new estate——' he smiled while she tidied her hair with some annoyance, 'remember that the size of the timbers, the thickness of the walls, even the slope of the stairs and so on have all been regulated by the aforementioned Act.'

She looked up at him. 'So a builder can't make up his own mind about those things?'

'He certainly can't. And what's more, he's got to show all his calculations to a local building inspector for approval. He has to take into account things like floor loading and wind loading—all in the interests of safety.'

'I begin to see,' she said slowly, 'why your grandfather handed over his business to you. You know so much about it, don't you?'

He smiled. 'If that's a compliment, even if it is an oblique one,' he bowed, 'many thanks. But knowing your opinion of me, it's probably more a statement of fact than an expression of admiration. Am I right?'

She looked down at her hands, refusing to answer.

'But you're learning too, aren't you? If I go on teaching you the basic requirements of the building industry, it won't be long before you know so much about it my grandfather and I might even consider offering you a partner-

128

ship.' His eyes grew mocking and he moved away. 'But that wouldn't do at all, would it? You'd want to reverse the process and knock down the houses we've built and put the trees back!'

He dropped into a chair and flung the safety helmet on the desk. He pushed his fingers through his thick brown hair and said casually,

'So you were out when I phoned last night. That's unusual for you. Where did you go—to Clare's place?'

'No.' She ran her forefinger lightly over the typewriter keys, glad that her back was towards him. 'I went out with Howard.'

He said sharply, 'I thought you didn't like him.'

'I don't, particularly. It's just that—well, he rather bulldozed me into it.'

'But you could have said "no, thanks".'

'Well, I didn't.' Her tone was petulant. 'I said "yes".'

'And I suppose when he asks you to marry him, you'll say "yes", justifying your answer by saying he "bulldozed you into it".'

Again she was silent.

'Do you like him any better now?'

'No. If anything, less.' He seemed to be waiting for her to explain. 'He—he kissed me.'

He got up and walked across to her, and leaned against the desk, facing her. The question came softly. 'And did you like it?'

She shivered. 'No. I hated it.'

'Perhaps you're cold.' She looked up, puzzled, and realised what he meant. 'Are you, Elise?'

She answered uncertainly, 'I—I don't know. I hope not, but——' She knew the worry was there in her eyes.

Slowly his hand came out and held her face, his lips followed and held her mouth. She did not back away, she did not flinch.

At last he lifted his head and took away his hand. 'No,

you're not cold. Whatever else you are, you aren't cold.'

He returned to his desk and sat down as though nothing had happened. She fought for composure and began to type, forcing herself to appear as calm and collected as he was. Why had he done it? To prove to her yet again how little she affected him?

He said, after a while, 'Easter's only ten days away. I'm going north to see my parents.'

She stopped typing and turned, saying tritely, 'Oh, that will be nice.'

He raised an eyebrow. 'For whom—you or me?'

She turned away from him. 'You know what I mean.'

'What will you do at Easter, Elise? Stay at home? Go out with Howard?'

She shrugged. 'Perhaps. Who knows?'

'No doubt,' he commented, and his cynicism stung her, 'it depends on how hard he pressurizes you, and whether or not he uses his "bulldozing" technique again.'

She did not reply.

He stood abruptly. 'Have you finished the work?'

'Not quite. Why?'

He put on his safety helmet and immediately pushed it to the back of his head. 'I have to go. Can you make your own way home?'

'Of course.'

He raised his hand and left her.

She worked on mechanically, her technical skill overriding her emotions and carrying her through to the end. She put the letters on Lester's desk to await his signature.

She swung her cardigan cape-like round her shoulders and a sleeve hit against the waste paper basket knocking it sideways on to the floor. The contents spilled out and she tutted and knelt down to scoop up the paper in handfuls, dropping it back into the basket.

Her eyes were caught by the words on a scrap of paper. The writing, which was somehow familiar, was carefully formed and rather feminine and seemed to be part of a letter which looked as if it had been ripped to pieces by angry fingers.

'Darling Lester,' it said, 'I'm writing to ask if you——' and there, tantalisingly, it stopped.

Still on her knees, she searched feverishly for more until piece by piece like a teasing jig-saw puzzle, she put the letter together again.

'Darling Lester,' she read again, 'I'm writing to ask if you will take me back. Please believe me when I say that I've never stopped loving you and would give everything I possess to see you again and feel your arms round me, holding me and loving me as you used to do.

'Is it possible for you to come north so that we could talk it over? Please write to me soon and say "yes". I miss you every hour of the day, darling. Yours for ever and ever, Nina.'

Slowly, hopelessly, Elise gathered up the torn pieces and dropped them back into the waste paper basket, watching them float and settle like giant flakes of snow. She gazed at them, frowning, wishing they would melt away before her eyes.

Well, at least she knew the worst. His ex-fiancée still loved him and wanted him back. She would be seeing him soon, wouldn't she, when he went north to see his parents? What did it matter that he had torn up her letter? Since the girl lived next door, they could hardly avoid meeting.

Elise thought of Nina's beauty and she remembered with piercing clarity the desolation which had driven Lester to the edge of brutality the night his engagement had ended.

Even if he had torn up Nina's letter, even if he did say monotonously and with apparent finality that he had put women out of his life, there was no doubt about it. Nina's wish would be granted—she would get Lester back.

Elise was alone in the house. She stood at the sitting-room

window watching the setting sun sinking in a wild cloud-scattered sky. The wind-racked branches of the trees bordering the pavement rose and dipped as if trying frantically to shake themselves free of the buds which were erupting all over them.

She was troubled by a restlessness that pawed at her like a dog demanding attention. The walls of the house imprisoned her body and stifled her mind. She felt a yearning for the woods that had gone, the rustling leaves, the crackle of twigs, birdsong, the scent of leaf-mould after rain.

The sense of loss, of deprivation returned and with it a fierce resentment, stronger than before, against those responsible for it. If those trees had been allowed to survive, they too would have been in bud, holding out hope in their uplifted branches, the promise of summer to come.

She thought about the thefts from the building site. They were getting worse, the local paper said. Things were disappearing at a faster rate. Windows, newly fitted, were being systematically smashed. Even the scaffolding fixed to the brickwork was being tampered with, causing a serious hazard to the workmen.

She wished she could be sure Phil Pollard was not behind it. Surely a man as sincere and honest as he was would be incapable of such action. But, another voice argued, someone who resented the development of that housing estate as much as he did might be capable of doing anything to impede its progress.

The restlessness within her became unbearable. She made up her mind—she would go out. She put on her blue anorak and tucked her trouser legs into long white boots. She slammed the front door behind her and, lowering her head, butted her way through the gale, which formed an almost tangible wall in front of her. She pitted her strength against it until it gave way before her dogged persistence.

An impulse had brought her out, an impulse which had contained the nucleus of an idea. 'Go to the building site,' it had said, 'wander round and try to find some clues which might help to establish the identity of the thief. Then Phil Pollard would be absolved from blame.'

The estate seemed deserted. She had expected that. A thief would remain hidden for as long as possible. He would not wander round openly as if he had every right to be there. He might even bring a van and leave it parked nearby, ready to be loaded with the stuff he had stolen.

A van! She thought of Phil Pollard's van, the one he used to deliver customer's goods. But she dismissed the thought. It would surely take an experienced criminal to be as well organised as that. And whatever else Mr. Pollard might be, he was not a criminal.

The wind raged and blustered through the half-built houses, whipping round stacks of timber, swooping over cement bags heaped into mounds and protected by tarpaulins with loose flapping corners. It played havoc with her hair and flirted with her jacket, making it billow out around her like an inflated balloon.

She picked her way over the scattered bricks and drain pipes and made for the shelter of a newly-completed house. There was glass in the windows, a neat front door and a double garage. She peered inside and admired the layout and the decorations, walked round the back and stood on tiptoe to look into the kitchen.

The equipment which had been installed was lavish and expensive. She envied the people who had had sufficient capital behind them to buy such a place. As she wandered over the land which would one day form the back garden, it came to her with a profound shock that the house occupied the ground where the hornbeam—her hornbeam—had stood.

She strolled round to the front again and as she emerged from the sideway, something warned her. Some primitive mechanism started ticking over in her brain, telling her of lurking danger. A prickle of primeval fear crawled up her spine, rippled across her neck and scraped over her scalp.

There was a noise, not an everyday sound that might be dismissed as meaningless, but a furtive shuffling which, lifted up and magnified by the clamour of the wind, made her body tingle with apprehension.

It was dusk now and her eyes strained to strip away the thin layer of darkness. There was the noise again and she peered into the increasing gloom in an effort to trace the source of it. Her eyes were caught and riveted by the shape of a dog, an Alsatian, standing a few feet away, staring at her. Its eyes were beady and menacing, its head was lowered, its ears pricked and rigid, its body tense and waiting.

Panic shortened her breath to gasps, she was encased in fear, mummified with fright. The dog snarled and drew back its lips. Its eyes were staring from its head, fur raised, body stiff and impatient and eager for blood.

Help, get help—the thought slipped stealthily, silently into her mind. Involuntarily she tore her eyes away from the dog's and looked up, straight into another pair of eyes— Lester's. He was standing at the door of the site office, watching, waiting for the dog—his guard dog—to spring and teach her a lesson.

He must have known all the time she was there. He must have been following her movements, observing her, waiting for her to start pilfering and thieving. A sob of horror that he could distrust her so racked her body. The dog, waiting for the slightest movement, sprang.

As its paws hit her shoulders, she screamed and went over backwards, twisting in her descent on to her side. Its teeth sought a hold, sank into the sleeve of her jacket, pulled and tore with all its strength. The jaws moved up-wards to the hood and wrenched and ripped and snarled. They moved again towards her neck and she put up her hands and screamed again.

134

Footsteps came pounding. There was a shout. The dog lifted its head and listened. A brick came hurtling past, missed the dog but frightened it. It fled away into the dusk.

Hands came out to help her, but she dragged herself upright and twisted away from them.

'Go away!' she screamed hysterically. 'It was your dog, your guard dog. You set him on me, you let him loose to come after me and tear me apart!'

'You're out of your mind, Elise. Do you think I would ever do such a thing?'

'You? You're capable of anything, even murder. Go away, I hate you!'

His hand shot out and grasped her arm and he dragged her towards him. She resisted with all her strength, but found his muscle power was greater than hers. She struggled nevertheless and he jerked her against his chest, trying to compel her to be still. She realised she had lost the battle and in her desperation found his hand, grasped it and lifted it towards her teeth.

He saw what she was doing, swore violently, took a handful of her hair and jerked back her head such force that she cried out. But he had freed the hand she had intended to bite.

'Come to your senses, woman! You're hysterical, you don't know what you're doing.' Limp now with exhaustion, she pulled away from him and stood abject, her head down, gasping for breath, her eyes full of tears from the pain of having her hair pulled.

She heard him mutter, 'And I tried to rouse you by calling you a mouse! I must have been crazy to summon your latent aggression out of limbo. I should have let it lie there forgotten and decently buried among all the other debris of your childhood.'

She put her hands to her face and her body shook with sobs. His arms went roughly round her and pulled her to him. She went because she had no strength to resist. When

135

he pushed her head down to his chest, she let it lie there while the rest of her body shook with the aftermath of terror. Gradually the shuddering passed and she lay still against him.

He said softly over head, 'Were you aware of what you were trying to do? Did you know you were trying to bite me again?' He lifted her face and she could hardly see him in the darkness, but he seemed to be smiling. 'Weren't you satisfied with the scar you've already given me—did you think it should be joined by another?'

'I'm sorry, Lester, I'm sorry,' was all she could say, and she sought the shelter of his chest again.

He held her close for a few more minutes, his hand stroking the hair he had pulled. Then he turned her gently and led her towards the site office. She went along beside him, her head still down. He switched on the light and sat her in a chair, finding another for himself.

'I wish I could give you a drink.' He looked round at the dusty filing cabinets, the wooden shelves crammed with box files. 'But I can't.' He waited for a few moments, then, 'Can you listen to me, Elise? I want to put the record straight. I want to make it perfectly clear that the dog which attacked you was not—repeat not—a guard dog. It was a stray I've seen prowling around for some time. It appeared to be harmless, so I've done nothing about it. But the gale and,' he smiled, 'the sight of you must have brought out the worst in it.' She sat silent, her head drooping. 'Do you believe me?'

She mumbled reluctantly, 'I suppose I shall have to.'

He looked at her clothes. 'Your jacket's a mess. I'm sorry about that. I'll buy you another.'

Her head came up and her look accused him. 'In doing so,' he said sharply, 'I am not admitting liability for the attack. I simply feel responsible because it occurred on this building site and because—because of our friendship in the past.'

She noted his carefully chosen words, implying that they were no longer friends. Well, she told herself miserably, it was true, wasn't it? She had said so herself often enough.

There was a long pause, then he asked as if he had had to force himself to do so, 'There's something I must know, Elise. Why were you wandering about on this estate?'

'I know what you're thinking,' she said resentfully, 'that I was going to steal something. Well, you're wrong.'

'I don't think that, Elise.' He was speaking gently. 'But I do think you may be shielding someone. Are you?'

She didn't answer. How could she? She could not be certain of Phil Pollard's innocence any more than he could.

'I think,' he went on, 'that it can't be ruled out that you might even be in league with him.' He leaned forward to take her hand, but she snatched it away. 'I'm sorry, Elise, but I had to say it.'

Again she was silent. 'I've come to these conclusions because of your initial objections to the development of the area...'

'And you think I'm now living a life of crime, carrying out a series of thefts calculated to hinder and even stop that development?'

'Not you personally, Elise, but Phil Pollard and his associates, with your support and encouragement.'

She began to cry again, she couldn't help it. That he should think so badly of her, that he should know so little about her he thought her capable of doing such a thing...

And yet she could not really defend herself because she could not be sure of Phil Pollard.

She stood up, prepared to leave. 'Why don't you go to the police and have me arrested as you once threatened? They'll get the truth out of me, won't they? With your connivance!'

A hard look narrowed his eyes and she realised that her stubborn attitude was incriminating her more and more. But there was nothing she could do about it. She was trapped in a web of her own making.

'I'll take you home,' he said curtly, but she ran from the
hut and was off the estate and well on her way before he
could stop her.

In the days that followed, she reverted to her old anti-social
ways. She shut herself in her room and sought consolation
in listening to music, clamping her headphones firmly on
her head and excluding the whole world. But it didn't seem
to work any more. Its powers of providing solace and
escape were waning. Thoughts of Lester kept intruding,
turning the music into a meaningless jumble of sounds, a
collection of discordant phrases.

One evening, a few days before Easter, Roland called her
to the telephone. 'A man,' he said, handing her the receiver.

She hoped it was Lester asking her to work for him
again, but it was Howard.

'Tomorrow evening,' he said, 'I take it you're free? If
the weather's fine, we could go for a run in the car.'

There he was again, assuming she was his for the asking.
But she put down her irritation like a mother dealing with a
fretful child and reluctantly agreed.

He would call for her, he said, arranging everything with
businesslike efficiency, at seven prompt. She half expected
him to say that he would confirm the appointment in writing, but rang off hurriedly before her sense of humour got
the better of her.

Idly, she put on another record and automatically adjusted the headphones. But her mind wandered back to
Lester and she decided she had had enough music for that
evening. Nevertheless, she heard the record through to the
end and as she listened, her sensitive ear detected a fault in
the equipment. It seemed to have developed an unpleasant
hum and she grew impatient and snatched off the headphones. Even her escape into music was denied her now.
The record player had let her down.

138

She told Phil Pollard next day.

'A loud hum, did you say? Could be a loose connection somewhere. Bring it into the shop this evening and I'll have a look at it for you.'

'Not this evening, Mr. Pollard.'

'Why?' he asked sharply. 'Got a date?'

She looked uncomfortable. 'Yes.'

'Who with? That Lester Kings?'

She laughed. 'Good heavens, no. Someone else.'

'Is it——' he stopped, hardly able to get the word out, 'serious?'

'I don't know. I—I don't think so.'

'Oh.' His voice was gruff. 'Well, bring it in tomorrow evening, then.' She said she would.

'Did I hear you say,' Clare said later, 'that you were going out tonight? Is it with that Howard Beale Lester was telling us about?'

She made a face. 'The same.'

'But if you don't like him, dearie, why torture yourself by going out with him?'

'Because I can't honestly think of any reason why I shouldn't. I know it sounds silly, but——'

'You're lonely. All right, but don't try to relieve your loneliness by getting involved with someone you can't stand. It might be a devil of a job getting uninvolved, dear. Some men won't take "no" for an answer, not even if you push them backwards out of the front door while you're saying it. I've a feeling your Howard might be one of them.'

'He's not "my" Howard, Clare.'

'Then say "no" now, Elise, and end it.'

Elise thought of Clare's advice when Howard called for her that evening. He urged her into the car and whisked her out into the countryside. All the way he uttered platitudes and banalities, saying tritely that 'spring was a lovely time of year' and making facetious remarks about 'young men's fancies' and looking at her slyly as he said it.

How could she 'end' it? There seemed to be something inevitable about it, like a rowing boat being swept out of control towards a roaring weir. This man beside her had every intention of making her the hostess in his house, the companion of his leisure-time activities, his partner at official functions and last of all, his wife and the mother of the children he planned to have. His determination was such that events were pulling her towards her ultimate destiny and she would soon go plunging helplessly over the edge.

He turned into a deserted country lane and pulled off on to the verge. 'I think it's time,' he said, 'we discussed our future. We are both aware of the reason for our acquaintance,' she was pleased he had not desecrated the word 'friendship' by using it, 'we both want a marriage partner and we both want companionship. I suggest,' he turned sideways and looked at her with less interest than a businessman would look at a girl who was applying for the post of his secretary, 'that we become engaged for a trial period, then get married. I also suggest that we do all this in the shortest possible time. I need a housekeeper and a wife,' she noted his order of priority, 'and you need someone to look after you and provide for you as you get older. What do you say?'

What could she say? Clare had said, 'say "no" and end it.'

'Well, I—I'm not sure ...' What was the matter with her? This was not saying 'no'. 'I don't think——'

'Don't think I'm giving you long enough? But I thought you were as eager as I was to find a life partner, a suitable life partner. There's surely no need for me to reveal my finances, to spell out the security I could offer you, the comforts, the status ...'

She wanted to scream, 'What about love?' but she merely said, 'You don't want a definite answer now, do you? I'd like to think about it for a few days——'

He sighed. 'All right, if you want to play coy. But I must make it quite clear that I'm not prepared to wait long.' He started the engine. 'Tell you what, next time we meet, I'll take you to see my house. Then you'll have concrete evidence of the excellence of my way of life.'

When he took her home he followed her into the house. She offered him coffee, but he refused it. Under the light in the hall, he caught her shoulders and kissed her. She found his lips as loathsome as before and had to exercise the greatest self-control to stop herself pushing him away. As she saw him out, Lester came down the stairs, saying sarcastically,

'A touching scene! Elise bids her boy-friend a passionate goodnight. Lucky man!'

'What are you doing here?' she demanded, sick at heart.

'I came for the express purpose of spying on your love life,' he said grinning. 'What else? All my motives are evil, according to you.'

'Oh, shut up,' she muttered, and went into the kitchen to make her father's cup of tea.

He followed and stood in the doorway. 'I owe you a new jacket.'

'You know that's not true.'

'All right, I'll start again. I'm going to buy you a new jacket.'

'No, thank you.'

'Now,' he went on as though she had not spoken, 'when shall we get it?'

' "We"?'

'Yes, we. Since I'm paying for it, I want to see what I'm spending my money on. Unless,' and innuendo coloured his tone, 'you want me to give you an open cheque such as a man might—er—give his mistress?'

She flushed at his deliberate insult and turned her face away. 'Tomorrow afternoon?' she asked dully.

'Yes, provided you don't object to my accompanying you in working clothes.'

'Not in the least. Will you pick me up or——?'

'Yes, I'll pick you up,' he said, and went out grinning.

She was ready when he called. He didn't get out of the van, he just sat and hooted. She ran out and he leaned across and opened the door for her.

'Keeps her appointment to the very second,' he commented sardonically. 'What more could Howard want in a wife?'

'Isn't that why you introduced us?' she snapped back. 'Because you considered us ideally suited?'

'That,' he said, glancing over his shoulder and pulling away from the kerb, 'is putting it a little strongly, but there's no doubt that he's in a position to give a woman everything she could possibly want.'

'Except one vital thing.'

He pulled up at the traffic lights and stared ahead. 'You're not talking about love again? If so, forget it. It's a myth.'

She edged away from him irritably.

'Are you going to marry him?'

'I—I don't know.'

His head came round. 'You don't mean you're actually considering it after all you've said about him?' He waited for a reply, but none came. 'So it seems that money, security, creature comforts—everything in fact that you've so scornfully dismissed—they've conquered after all?'

The lights changed and he drove on.

'It's not that,' she said slowly, 'it's—oh, it doesn't matter.'

'It's what? His bulldozing technique?'

She shrugged. How could she tell him that it frightened her to go out with Howard because he seemed to have some power over her, drawing her after him like the Pied Piper drew the children?

'Go on, Elise.' His voice was surprisingly gentle. 'I'm listening.'

She shook her head. 'You're the last person I could pour out my heart to.'

'Thanks for that.' Now his voice was sharp. 'Anyway, I don't see why not. You've known me long enough.'

'What difference does that make? You still laugh at me, you never take me seriously.'

'That, my sweet Elise,' his hand came down and covered hers as it rested on her knee, 'is where you're wrong. I take you very seriously, especially when you tell me you hate me.'

Her eyes stared despondently at the fashion stores and supermarkets they were passing.

'While I remember,' Lester broke into her thoughts, 'I'd be glad of some help in the office tomorrow. Could you oblige? I'm going north in a couple of days, as you know, and I'd like to get my work up to date before I go.'

Her heart jerked with pleasure. It was the request she had been waiting for. 'Yes, I'll help you.'

'Good. I'll see you there. Be ready for a couple of hours' hard work. Now, where are we buying this jacket?'

'I thought of trying Wilfred Frenley's shop. He usually has a good selection.'

'Old man Frenley? Is he still in business? He should have retired long ago. He's almost in my grandfather's generation.' He looked thoughtful as he reversed into a parking space. 'Wasn't he one of those who joined your protest meeting that day in the woods?'

'Your memory's a bit too good.'

'Isn't it?' he joked. 'Come on, get out.' He gave her a push that was none too gentle and she scrambled out of the van.

'This,' he said, as he walked beside her to the car park, 'should be an interesting encounter.'

She said, looking up at him anxiously, 'Don't say anything to him about it, Lester.'

He merely patted her on the shoulder and smiled. He followed her into the shop. It was dim inside, as if the proprietor was economising on electricity. Lester shaded his eyes ironically as though shielding them from a dazzling light. The counter was brown and wooden. There were no modern fitments and the atmosphere was such that the twentieth century might not yet have arrived. But the stock was surprisingly up to date, the quality good and the choice wide.

Lester leaned on his elbow against the counter, crossing his booted legs nonchalantly and drumming his fingers restlessly on the wooden surface. Elise left his side and found the rack displaying the type of jacket she wanted. She flipped her hand along them looking for her size.

'Yes, sir,' murmured a low-pitched, obsequious voice from the shadows, 'what can I do for you?'

Lester indicated Elise with a movement of his hand. 'The lady wants a jacket.'

Wilfred Frenley, rotund in shape and shrewd in judgment, moved ponderously round the counter and asked Elise what she required. The sweep of his arm included the entire contents of the shop. 'Help yourself, my dear; help yourself. Try on as many as you like. All the garments are priced.'

'Since I'm paying, Elise,' Lester said, 'there's no need to go for the cheapest. Get the best. Otherwise Howard might disown you.'

She gave him a look, but he grinned and leaned back against a pillar, arms folded, legs crossed, as though prepared for a long wait. There were no other customers.

'Tell me, Mr. Frenley,' Lester said, the light of battle in his eyes, 'what do you think of the new Kings' estate going up where Dawes Hall woods used to be?'

Mr. Frenley carefully and quite unnecessarily rearranged some boxes of handkerchiefs displayed on the counter. His

144

eyes, astute and discerning, flickered over Lester's working clothes.

'You've come from there, sir? You're connected with the firm?'

'Er—yes. I'm directing operations.'

Wilf Frenley's eyes searched his face. 'You wouldn't be Mr. Kings' grandson, would you?' Then his face broke into a broad smile. 'Of course you are. I remember you when you were a lad. Bit of a scamp you were, too, if I remember rightly. Always climbing those trees and getting into trouble with your mother.' His smile faded.

Lester guessed the reason and followed it up. 'Pity,' he commented, leading the old man on, 'we had to cut them down, wasn't it?'

'Ah, it was now.' His tone was cautious. He turned a professional eye on Elise, who was pulling on an anorak. 'But,' his smile reappeared, 'I was only saying to my good lady the other day what a good job you were making of it.'

Elise pulled the fastener up to her neck and asked Lester to move away from the pillar. 'You're covering up the mirror.'

He lifted himself upright and looked her over. 'Red. I like that. The colour suits you. Brightens you up, gives you a certain—something. Are you having it?'

She answered uncertainly, 'It's a bit expensive.'

'I told you, it doesn't matter.' He drew out his wallet.

'Do you mind, Lester, if I looked at some trousers while I'm here? I need a new pair.'

'Red,' he asked hopefully, 'to go with the jacket?'

'There are the trousers, miss,' Mr. Frenley said. 'There's red among them. They'd make a nice outfit, as the gentleman says.'

Lester turned back to the old man. 'So you think we're making a good job of the building?'

'Well, there's good estates and bad, you know. Now

145

yours is good.' He warmed to his subject. 'First, the houses, they're good quality, you can see that at a glance. Better than your old grandfather used to build in the old days, if I may say so.'

Lester nodded. 'I've seen to that.'

'Another thing, they're spaced well apart. You've saved some trees, too.'

'And we intend planting some more, to replace the diseased elms we had to cut down.'

He turned briefly to see if Elise had heard and smiled at the surprise in her eyes.

'So you think, Mr. Frenley,' he went on, 'that all in all the estate blends in with its surroundings? That, of course, is why we employed an architect in the first place. He planned the entire estate, and told us how many houses we could comfortably fit in without spoiling the look of the area.'

Mr. Frenley nodded. 'Something else we noticed— you've respected people's privacy. The estate's screened from the road. There's an estate a few miles away from here that you might call garish. It sticks out a mile from its surroundings. The houses are ugly-looking and put you off. But inside, I'm told, they're good. So you can't tell by appearances, can you?'

'No, just as you can't judge a woman by her looks.' Lester turned. 'Isn't that right, Elise?'

She ignored his provocation and stood in front of the mirror holding a pair of trousers against herself.

'Well, Mr. Frenley,' Lester returned to the old man, 'it's nice to know you don't object to the building site any more. But there's someone who does and I wish I knew who it was.'

'Yes, I saw from the local paper you were having trouble with thieves and pilferers.'

Trust Lester, Elise thought angrily, replacing the trousers and searching for a pair that would fit her, to try to

146

lead the old man on to giving him some clues.

'I remember,' Mr. Frenley was saying, 'a group of noisy youngsters at the meeting that day.'

'Yes,' Lester answered grimly, 'my grandfather had good reason to remember them, too. After the meeting they broke the office windows at his house.' Mr. Frenley tutted and Lester fiddled with a discarded price tag. 'You—er—think it could be them—with someone bribing them, perhaps?'

Now he's putting words into the man's mouth, Elise thought, glaring at Lester's broad, uncaring back. She went to the counter and held out a pair of trousers.

'You could be right,' Mr. Frenley mumbled, 'you could be right.' He took the trousers from Elise. 'These, miss? Red, to match the jacket. You've made the right choice.'

'My word,' commented Lester, 'this surely is the event of a lifetime. She's actually taken my advice!'

'Shall I add them up together, miss?' Mr. Frenley asked.

Elise opened her mouth to say, 'No, separately,' when Lester said, 'Yes, please. I'm paying.'

'But, Lester,' Elise protested, 'I didn't mean——'

He held up his hand to silence her and gave Mr. Frenley a handful of notes. The man looked up, smiling benevolently.

'Are you two getting ——?'

'No,' said Lester firmly, 'we're not. We're just good friends.'

Elise turned away sharply, and Mr. Frenley said, 'Oh,' but it was the way he said it that annoyed her.

Lester taunted, as he helped her into the van, 'Now the tongues will start wagging. I've bought you some clothes. If it gets round to Howard, he might even challenge me to a duel in defence of your honour!' He pulled out into the main road, overtaking a learner-driver. 'And,' he said quietly, his voice holding an odd anticipation, 'may the best man win.'

CHAPTER IX

ELISE wore her new red outfit that evening. She had to admit that Lester was right—it did 'do something' for her. No one, not even Lester, could dismiss her as a 'mouse' in that outfit. She wished he could see her in it.

Roland gave her a lift to Phil Pollard's and carried the hi-fi equipment into the shop before going on to Clare's.

Phil's eyes opened wide. 'My, you look pretty!' He opened up the record player on the counter. 'Let me see, didn't I think it might be a loose connection?' With the care and respect of a fanatical hi-fi enthusiast he turned the record player upside down and removed the base.

'I'll have to unscrew the circuit board and have a look underneath.' He eased the board out of the case and peered at the maze of wires and components, lifting them and probing with gentle fingers. 'Ah, I see it, there's a wire come loose and it's been touching the base. That would cause the hum. Won't take long to repair it.'

He took out his soldering iron and plugged it in to the mains. Twenty minutes later, the wire had been re-connected and the record player reassembled. 'There, that didn't take long, did it?' He looked at her, doubt and hope mingling in his eyes. 'Are you going home now, or——?'

She nodded. 'Home.'

'Then—would you come out with me on that drive we've never had? We could stop for a coffee somewhere? Only for half an hour or so, Elise?' There was a pleading lift to his voice that she did not have the heart to resist. She nodded. 'Good, good,' he said, and carried the hi-fi equipment to the car. 'I'll take you home afterwards.'

His car was waiting at the kerb and he opened the boot and lowered the equipment into it. As she stood on the pavement waiting for him to let her into the car, a Kings' van approached.

'No,' she willed, straining to see the driver's face, 'not Lester. It mustn't be Lester.'

The van slowed to a standstill a few feet behind Phil's car. The driver was staring at her as though he could not believe his eyes.

'Don't,' Elise wanted to shout. 'It's not true what you're thinking, Lester. I'm not in league with Phil. We're not working together. We aren't responsible for those thefts. Please, please believe me!'

But the van was pulling out and moving on, and she had not spoken a word. As he drew alongside Phil's car, the look which Lester turned upon her ripped her into tiny pieces like a torn-up letter and scattered her to the winds.

With appeal in her eyes, with the disavowing shake of her head, she tried to declare her innocence and plead for his understanding. But he dismissed her pleading with contempt and she knew she had failed.

Phil took her for a drive and they had coffee at a pleasant roadside hotel on the way home. She thanked him as he carried her record player into the house, and he in turn thanked her sincerely for her company.

'Another evening, perhaps?' he suggested, full of hope.

'That would be nice,' she answered, her voice falsely bright.

Later, when the phone rang, she guessed who it was, and her hand grew moist as she gripped the receiver. 'Elise?' Lester's curt tone told her the worst.

She whispered, 'Yes.'

'You can forget about helping me tomorrow. In fact, I shall not require your services again. I'll send you what I owe you. I'm getting someone else to do the work, someone I can trust.'

He rang off before she had a chance to reply. Two days later, he went away.

Howard kept his promise. He took her out to dinner, then

produced his house like a conjuror taking a rabbit out of a hat.

'This is it,' he said with pride, as if he were inviting her into a royal palace.

She could not deny its attractions. She had to concede that as a residence, it was certainly desirable. It was furnished and equipped on a scale that was both lavish and showy and it was plain that the woman he would take for a wife would have to be gracious and sophisticated to go with it.

What puzzled her as she strolled round, dutifully admiring everything she saw, was why he thought she possessed such qualities. Was he so blind that he could not see that her very nature would not allow her to be those things? Or did he think that with a little tuition from him, she would develop into the perfect hostess he required?

They returned to the lounge, with its great picture window overlooking a large and impossibly neat back-garden. He put a drink into her hand and told her to sit down. What did she think of the place? He wanted to know, as proud of it as if it were something he had physically created himself, like the mother of a child who had proved to be a prodigy.

She praised it extravagantly, failing to realise that he would regard this as a sign of her acceptance of him as a husband. That he had taken it that way occurred to her suddenly as he removed the empty glass from her hand and sat himself as close to her as he could physically get.

His arms went round her, he pushed her back against the cushions and began to make love to her with as much method and attention to detail as he gave to his work. It was a passionless, mechanical approach which required nothing of her but toleration and a stoical endurance. As a first experience of the desires of a man, it was horrifying and repellent.

But she did not see it that way. She thought she should able to respond, that there was something lacking in herself.

She began to despair. At last, to her infinite relief, he stopped.

'Yes, well,' he said, putting his handkerchief to his brow, 'it will come in time, it will come.'

He took her home at her request, and when she left him outside the house he said, 'Soon we must get a ring. We must make it official.'

She made her father's cup of tea and he came down from his room looking tired and in need of comfort. But, as he lowered himself wearily into the armchair, he saw that his daughter was in some distress and was as much in need of comfort as he was.

'What's wrong, love?' His tone was deliberately brisk as if giving the impression that he did not want to force her confidence.

She shook her head.

'Been out with Howard?' She nodded. 'Anywhere exciting?'

She shrugged. 'To his house.' There was a short silence, then, 'I think he tried to sell it to me, with himself thrown in as a special offer.'

Her father laughed, as if glad of the chance to ease the tension.

'Dad,' she said, then stopped. She looked at his impassive face, took comfort and went on, 'He wants me to marry him.' Another pause. 'And I don't know what to say.'

He took some time to answer, so long in fact that she went on, 'He's got a beautiful house, plenty of money, a good position. By nature he seems to be stable, solid, safe ...' Her voice trailed away.

At last her father spoke. 'That's all very well, love, but you don't marry bricks and mortar, or cash. You marry a man, not his possessions or position. What you must ask yourself is, do you fit in with each other intellectually, do you share the same interests, does the world stop turning when you're together? You know what I mean, Elise. Does he attract you physically? When he's away from you do you feel you're only half alive?' She was shaking her head so vigorously that he stopped asking questions and answered hers.

'Then it's no, love, three thousand times "no".' He sat forward, his hands clasped. 'Look, Elise, don't ever think I want you to go. This house is yours as well as mine. Don't think, either, that I want you to stay. If ever you found someone you loved—and I mean loved—you're as free to go as those birds flying about out there are free to migrate when the time comes.'

'But, Dad,' she spoke as though the words were clinging to her like a frightened child, 'I—I think I'm cold. I don't think I'd make any man a good wife.' She hid her face in her hands, trying to shut out Lester's face.

Her father came to her and put his hand on her head. 'My dearest girl, you're talking the most arrant nonsense. You're as warm and loving and sweet-natured and responsive as your mother was. She was the most wonderful woman—and wife—a man could ever hope to have. To say I miss her would be the grossest understatement of all time.'

'I'm sorry,' she whispered through her fingers. 'I'm sorry to have burdened you with my troubles. But thanks for listening—and for helping.'

He bent down and kissed the top of her head. He said, as he went to the door, 'That's what fathers are for, isn't it?'

She was in her bedroom, lost to the world the following evening, with her stereo headphones clamped firmly over her ears, when Roland walked in, pulling Clare behind him.

'We're engaged,' he said, when Elise had freed herself from wires and flex, 'and we're making it official.'

The two girls embraced and laughed and Roland said, 'We're thinking of having a party to celebrate, just a few drinks and savouries.' He looked at his sister expectantly. 'Tomorrow. I know it's short notice, but could you cope?'

Clare held on to his arm. 'I told you, darling, I'll see to the food.'

Elise said, 'Let's both do it, Clare.'

So they agreed that Clare would arrive early and help with the preparations.

'Who's coming?' Elise asked.

'A few of Roland's colleagues,' Clare said, 'and their partners. One or two friends of mine. What about you, Elise? You can't be the odd one out, without a partner. Can't you ask Lester?'

'He's away,' Elise said shortly.

'Anyway,' said her brother, 'they're sworn enemies, so that's no good. What about Howard?' Elise made a face. 'You must have a partner, Elise.'

'Yes, she must,' Clare laughed, 'otherwise I can see what will happen—she'll dash away half-way through and lock herself in here.'

'All right,' Elise said grudgingly, 'I suppose I'll have to ask Howard.'

When she phoned him he accepted with alacrity. 'I'll bring some drink. I've just had a thought—what about announcing our engagement at the same time?'

She felt trapped. The bulldozer was advancing on her, getting nearer and nearer. 'Oh—er—not yet, Howard.'

'What do you mean—not yet? How much longer do you intend to fool about, pretending "no's" the answer when I know very well it's "yes"?'

'It's—it's just,' she had to think quickly, 'it's just that it's Roland and Clare's party, their engagement, and it doesn't seem right to try and make it ours too, does it?'

He sighed. 'Have it your way. We'll have a party of our own, if that's what you want.'

Next day Clare arrived soon after lunch. 'Look at the ring your wonderful brother's given me.' Two diamonds

153

sparkled in an attractive platinum setting.

'Lovely!' Elise exclaimed. 'My brother's got good taste in more ways than one.'

'That,' said Clare, pulling up her sleeves, 'is blatant flattery. But I'm lapping it up. Now, let's get down to it.

'I wish,' she said suddenly as they worked, 'you were as happy as I am. I'd like to do for you what you did for me.' When Elise looked puzzled, she said, 'I wish *I* had a brother I could introduce you to!'

Elise laughed. 'Then we really would all be one big happy family!'

'Isn't there—anyone you like well enough to want to marry?'

Elise answered with a careful laugh. 'I doubt if I'm the marrying kind, Clare. Anyway, it takes two, remember! I think there must be something about me that freezes a man up. I just haven't got what it takes.'

'Stop under-estimating yourself, dear.' She patted Elise on the back. 'Just wait until Auntie Clare gets going on you this afternoon. You won't recognise yourself.' She said quietly, after a while, 'I thought the same about myself—until I met my husband. When you meet the person you want to marry, you somehow find in yourself all the qualities you thought you hadn't got.'

'Does it still hurt to talk about him, Clare?'

She shook her head. 'Not now. Our marriage was wonderful while it lasted, which wasn't very long. When he died, I thought the end of the world had come, but now——' She brightened. 'I've told Roland all about it and he understands. I'll say it again, and you can't stop me— you've got a wonderful brother, Elise!'

They went upstairs laughing. Clare's dress was yellow and sleeveless and she had bought it specially for the occasion. She put it on and made up her face and combed her long black hair, then turned to Elise. 'What are you wearing?'

154

'Something that's been hanging in the cupboard since I bought it months ago. I've never had any reason to wear it before.'

'Well, now's the time to give it an airing. Come on, show Auntie.'

Elise searched in the wardrobe and brought out the dress. 'M'm, looks promising,' said Clare. 'Put it on.'

The fabric was summer-weight and patterned in a mixture of red, grey and yellow. It was long-sleeved and buttoned high to the neck, following her figure closely to the waist, where it was pulled in by a wide, silver-buckled belt, then it hung in soft folds to the hem.

'Wow!' said Clare. 'Very fetching, very effective. Should put Howard in the mood to propose.'

Elise looked startled. 'Then I'd better take it off again!'

Clare laughed and said, 'Don't you dare! I've never seen you look so good. Now for your face.'

Ten minutes later, Clare stood back and admired her efforts. 'You're a different girl. You never know, one of Roland's friends might take a fancy to you and snatch you from under Howard's nose!'

The guests began to drift in and Harold Lennan hovered uncomfortably in the background. Elise detected in his eyes the urge to escape and she smiled reassuringly at him.

She whispered, full of sympathy because she shared his solitary nature, 'Go upstairs if you want to, Dad. Roland and Clare won't mind.'

He looked pathetically pleased. 'Well, dear, if you think they won't be offended ... I never was a very social animal.' He made for the stairs, saying over his shoulder, 'Call me if you want me.'

Howard came, stolid as ever. As he stepped in the door, he pulled two bottles from under his jacket. Clare opened her arms to receive them, crying 'Manna from heaven!' and disappeared with them into the kitchen.

'Hallo, Elise,' Howard said, and kissed her. His eyes

155

were tinged with surprise, but they nevertheless appraised and approved. He seemed to be silently commending her for dressing so suitably for the role of hostess she was about to play—practising, as it were, for the part she would be called upon to act in his own home, when she became his wife.

After that, wherever she went, he followed. Even when she went into the kitchen, he waited at the door until she came out again. She could not shake him off. He clung like adhesive and she could find no solvent with which to remove him.

Clare stood on tiptoe and whispered to Roland, 'Can't you help your poor sister? Howard's shadowing her everywhere she goes. Couldn't you ask Rob over there,' she indicated a young man sitting alone, 'to act as a decoy?'

Roland nodded. He called out, 'Elise, just a moment,' and before Howard knew what was happening, she was following her brother.

Roland murmured to Rob, who grinned and made room for Elise to sit beside him. She squeezed into the small space, feeling tongue-tied and embarrassed but glad to do anything which would help her escape from her pursuer.

Rob whispered to her like a conspirator. It was mostly nonsense, but she managed to look interested and absorbed and even laughed at his jokes. But the ruse did not succeed for long. A possessive hand descended to her shoulder like that of a policeman about to make an arrest.

Rob's eyes sympathised. He made a face behind his empty glass. 'I've done my best,' he murmured. 'Now it's over to you. Sorry, chum.'

He got up and moved away, abandoning her to her fate. Howard remained where he was, his fingers clamping her firmly to him, like a child who would not be parted from a cherished toy.

The phone rang and Roland answered it. He came across the room and whispered, 'That was Lester. He's back a day

156

early, so I asked him over.' He saw her dismay and wrongly interpreted it as disapproval. He reprimanded in a big-brother tone, 'I had to ask him, Elise. Anyway, it's my party and he'll be my guest, not yours.'

Now she knew Lester was coming, her tension mounted. Over the laughter and the talk, her ears picked up the sound of every vehicle that passed the house. When at last a car slowed down and stopped outside, she had a mad desire to run up to her bedroom and lock herself in.

But Howard's hand, still fastened to her shoulder, kept her beside him. When the doorbell rang, she pressed her moist palms together and tried to get up. But as she did so the sitting-room door opened and she flopped down again.

Lester's eyes swept round the room and settled on her. There was no smile on his face, no look of pleasure at see-ing her again. She knew instinctively that he still had not forgiven her for her supposed association with Phil Pollard.

Howard moved to occupy the chair Rob had vacated. His glass was full again and it occurred to Elise that he might be drinking more than was good for him.

Roland pushed Lester into the centre of the room. 'Another friend of mine,' he shouted above the din, 'Lester Kings. You'll all have to make your own introductions.'

'Lester!' Clare held out her hand and he pulled her to-wards him.

'Congratulations,' he said, kissing her cheek, and every-one applauded.

'Wow, I like your outfit, Lester,' she said, admiring the multi-coloured shirt he was wearing. 'And that tie!' She hid her eyes. 'It blinds me!' She pointed to the wide patterned leather belt round his waist. 'And look at this. Talk about trendy!'

'What's happened, Lester,' Roland joked, 'been indulg-ing your libido while you were away?'

'Or,' commented Clare, 'perhaps you've found another girl-friend?'

157

'Not on your life!' said Lester. 'I told you, I've renounced women.'

Everyone laughed. Rob called out, 'Then you're going
the wrong way about it, Lester. In that outfit you'll have
them grovelling at your feet.'

'Then the pleasure will be all the greater,' his eyes held
malice as they sought Elise, 'in throwing them aside, one by
one.'

'We have a Casanova in our midst,' one of the men called
out. 'Ladies, be warned, lock up your hearts and keep your
distance from this hard-hearted brute!'

The man in question listened intently as Roland whispered in his ear, his gaze resting first on Elise, then on
Howard beside her. As he listened, his eyes narrowed with a
spiteful pleasure and he nodded.

He strolled towards them, thumbs hooked into his trouser
pockets. He might have been drawing an imaginary sword
from its scabbard in readiness for a duel-to-the-death with
an avowed enemy.

He stood on the raised tiled hearth, thus adding an inch
or two to his already towering height, and propped a
shoulder against the wall above the fireplace.

'Hallo, Elise,' he said, his eyes caressing, 'missed me,
sweetie, while I've been away?'

She coloured deeply, suspecting him of the worst possible motives. Howard spluttered in the act of committing
the liquid in his glass to his throat. Lester did nothing to
help him. He waited until the man had recovered, then
went on,

'Did you go out over the holiday, sweetie?'

She shrugged, knowing he did not require an answer.
The question was merely a preliminary to what was to
follow.

'You didn't? Well, I'm not really surprised. You know,
Howard,' his eyes rested sadistically on the other man, 'I
know this girl almost as well as I know myself, but what

158

I've never been able to understand is why such an attractive girl should want to keep hiding herself away.' He bent down whispered, his tone falsely confiding. 'Do you know what her favourite occupation is?'

Howard shook his head dumbly.

'Listening to music—classical music.' He paused while Howard winced. 'But that's not all, my dear chap. She listens to it on headphones, stretched out on her bed—well, that's how I've found her every time I've gone up to her bedroom, which is pretty often.'

He waited again, while Howard flushed a dull red and digested this piece of information. Elise looked at the speaker as if she would like to get her hands to his throat. She could not deny his assertions, because in essence they were true. It was only in the context in which he was presenting them that they were false.

'You know,' Lester murmured, putting his fingers under her chin with a gesture that could have been born of intimacy, 'you may think this girl's a quiet little mouse, but take it from me, as I know to my cost she's really a vicious tigress at heart. She bit me once. I still bear the scar. I could show it to you, but,' he released her chin looked around and lowered his voice, 'in the circumstances, it would be a bit embarrassing.'

'Lester!' She had to stop him. 'Will you be quiet! You know very well that what you're saying——'

'Is not for other people's ears. All right, my sweet, I'll keep our secret.'

'*Please*, Lester!' It was a cry from the heart and it should have touched his compassion, but it seemed that he possessed no such quality any more.

'Those clothes I bought you recently, pet. Have you worn them yet?' He grinned diabolically. 'They seem to have caused quite a stir. Old man Frenley passed the message round that we were—er—"walking out" together and that I was buying you presents. And according to the gossipmongers, when a man does that for a woman, well ...!' He laughed as though he enjoyed the thought. 'Now it seems to be generally accepted that we're having an affair. That, together with the stories put round about us by my former landlady, really has given us both a reputation!'

Howard appeared to be finding it difficult to breathe. He ran a shaking finger round the inside of his shirt collar and loosened his tie as if it had been choking him.

Elise said, now beside herself with anger, 'It can't be true, Lester. You're making it all up.'

'I assure you, my sweet,' he injected the endearment with a deep familiarity, 'I'm telling you the truth. Ask Mrs. Dennis—she told me about the rumour as soon as I arrived home this afternoon.'

Howard stood up, staggering sideways as if he had been dealt a punishing blow. He muttered thickly as he moved away,

'Think I'll get myself another drink.'

As soon as he had gone, Elise gripped Lester's arm, but he shook off her hold. 'Sorry, *sweetie*, someone's calling me.'

He had achieved his object—he had vanquished his opponent, verbally slain him in fact. The prize was his for the asking. But he did not choose to ask. He turned his back on her instead and sauntered across the room to talk to a pretty young redhead who was sitting alone.

Well, Elise tried to console herself, at least he had done something for her—he had given her a respite from Howard's surveillance. She moved her eyes stealthily sideways to see if Howard was watching, but he was tossing back a drink and helping himself to another like a man trying to drown his sorrows. She seized her chance of freedom and made a dash for the kitchen, rejoicing in her sudden emancipation like an escaped prisoner scaling a wall and dropping down the other side.

She made some fresh coffee and was so engrossed she did

160

not hear a sound behind her. But something alerted her— she was being watched.

It couldn't be, it must not be Howard. She spun round. It was Lester. She smiled with sheer relief. He did not smile back. The touch of familiarity in his manner had gone as if it had never been. His expression was cold, his eyes likewise as he said, 'I must congratulate you on your appearance. I've never seen you looking so attractive.'

She coloured. 'Thanks, but it was mostly Clare's doing.'

'Yes, I thought I could detect Clare's handiwork.' He looked her over closely. 'But there's something else about you, some quality which no amount of cosmetics could instil in you.' She was silent, concentrating on making the coffee. 'Anyone would think,' he went on casually, 'that you were in love. Are you?'

That was a question she could not answer.

'How's Phil Pollard?'

Now she could see how his mind was working. 'I've been on holiday. We don't go back to work until tomorrow.'

'So you haven't seen him?'

'Of course I haven't seen him.' She lowered the coffee pot on to the tray. 'He's my employer, not my friend.'

'No? You went out with him last week. I saw you.'

'That,' she answered crisply, 'was purely business.'

'Of course.' His cynical smile showed that he had not believed a word of it.

He blocked the doorway. 'Excuse me, please,' she said. 'I want to take this tray into the other room.'

He didn't move. He said, 'I'll take it. Give it to me.'

She tried to push away his fingers as they met hers round the edges of the tray, but she could not push away his eyes as they met hers over the top of it. There seemed to be a question in his, a message which she struggled to read, but it was in a language which she had never been taught to understand. She was transfixed, she moved her lips to whisper his name, to ask him what he was trying to say. She felt it was of the utmost importance that she should know. But the sardonic twist to his smile stopped her as effectively as a hand slapped across her mouth.

Humiliated that she had allowed herself to imagine a message that was not there—had she really been stupid enough to believe that he was telling her he loved her?—she gave him the tray, and he acknowledged his victory with a mocking bow.

By the time they reached the others, she had recovered her poise. 'Thanks,' she said coldly, taking the tray again, 'but I could have carried it just as easily myself.'

He raised an eyebrow at her ingratitude and strolled away. She walked round the room offering people coffee, pouring it out and distributing it, her mind busy all the time trying to discover the meaning of the silent message in Lester's eyes.

Roland called her name and pushed his way across the room, pulling Clare behind him. 'They want to drink a toast to us, Elise. Don't you think we should call Dad? He might be upset if we didn't ask him to join us.'

She nodded, put down the tray and looked furtively round the room for Howard. But someone was talking to him and she sent the man a silent vote of thanks. Even so, as she climbed the stairs, she glanced behind, unable to believe that Howard was not following her.

She tapped on her father's door and went in. 'Dad,' she said, and stopped. Lester was lounging across a corner of the table, talking. She had interrupted what had sounded like a technical discussion.

Lester raised an eyebrow. 'You surely aren't looking for me?'

'Of course not.'

'No, I thought you weren't. You never did like me enough to chase after me, did you?'

Harold Lennan laughed. 'Never take a woman's words or deeds at their face value, Lester. When she says "no" she

162

means "yes", and when she says "go away" she means "come and get me"!'

Elise frowned. Her father was too near the truth for comfort.

But Lester shook his head. 'Not this girl. She means what she says, don't you, Elise?'

'That's where you're wrong, boy. My daughter's no different from other women.'

'Dad,' said Elise, firmly changing the subject, 'you're wanted downstairs. They're going to drink a toast to Roland and Clare.'

'Right.' With his hands against the table, he pushed himself to his feet. 'Heaven knows, I've waited long enough for my son to get himself engaged.'

They went down, Elise leading the way.

'I only hope,' grunted Harold, 'that my daughter doesn't keep me waiting this long before she hooks the man of her choice.'

As they joined the party, Howard, who had personally chosen himself to fill that vacancy was wearing the expression of an abject dog. On seeing his future mate enter the room, his eyes strained at the leash as he made frantic attempts to get to her before the toasts were drunk. But she was hemmed in on the one side by her father and on the other by Lester, and as there were people all round them, Howard's frenzied efforts to reach her were doomed from the start.

Lester saw his predicament and grinned. 'Your boyfriend seems to be suffering from chronic frustration,' he whispered. 'His abortive attempts to get at you touch my heart.'

A toast was drunk to the happy couple, but that, apparently, was not enough. Having started to lift their glasses, everyone cried out for more.

'Who next?' someone asked. 'The lady of the house?'

Clare took him up. 'Yes, let's drink to Elise.'

163

'Who's the lucky man?' Rob asked, winking wickedly at Elise and looking at Howard.

'Come on,' Clare said, staring pointedly at Lester, 'somebody volunteer. There's an attractive, heart-whole young lady standing there waiting to be claimed. Any offers?'

Howard became violent in his attempts to take his rightful place beside her, but the pressure of the other guests still held him prisoner.

Lester eyed him maliciously and grinned down at Elise. 'They're all looking at us, darling, so smile sweetly.'

There was a burst of laughter and someone chortled, 'Casanova's been caught at last. Let's drink to him and the clever lady who did it.'

So they drank a toast to Elise and Lester. But she would not acknowledge them. 'Tell them the truth, Lester,' she pleaded, raising herself on to her toes and whispering in his ear.

'Drink, girl,' he whispered back, 'don't spoil their fun.'

So, reluctantly, she drank. Then someone proposed a toast to the father of the bridegroom-to-be and Harold smiled, tolerating with good humour the spotlight that fell on him for a few passing moments.

When it was over, Elise moved away from Lester's side. He did not attempt to stop her.

'I'm off, love,' Harold murmured in his daughter's ear. 'You don't mind?'

She gave him an affectionate push and he returned thankfully to the solitude of his room.

For the remainder of the evening, she moved amongst the guests acting the gracious hostess which, if nothing else, took her out of Howard's reach, although he dogged her footsteps most of the time.

When she did allow herself now and then to glance at Lester, she found his eyes upon her and he smiled sardonic-

164

ally as he watched her vain attempts to elude her pursuer.

In fact, Lester's efforts to put Howard off her scent seemed to have misfired. The man was more persistent than ever. Elise could not understand it, but it was almost as though Lester's hints of a liaison between them had made Howard even more possessive towards her.

When the party was nearly over, he was still sticking like a limpet. Others began to leave, but he stayed on. Elise went into the kitchen to start the washing up, but he hovered in the doorway. She eyed his position, trying to assess her chances of getting past him unmolested and fleeing up to her father's room.

She dried her hands and, making some excuse about having a word with Roland, she pushed through to the hall, but he lunged forward and caught her, propelling her backwards into the dining-room and shutting the door.

His arms trapped her. 'I've got you now,' he growled, 'and this time you're not getting away.' He muttered indistinctly against her hair, 'So you're not the sweet little innocent you've been pretending to be, eh? You've been leading me on with your "coyness", have you? I'll teach you to play with me!'

His mouth tried in vain to settle on hers, but her evasive tactics were too effective for him in his fuddled state. He started to make violent love to her. He was awkward and bungling and as he forced her back against the table, she writhed and twisted and managed by sheer persistence to get a hand free, using it to give him a stinging slap across the cheek.

He let her go at once, his face red, his chest heaving. He was incoherent with rage. With his hand to his scarlet cheek, he swung out of the room, stumped down the hall and slammed out of the house.

She slumped into a chair and covered her face. She was shaking. When someone walked in and closed the door, she didn't look up.

'What's the matter?' asked Lester.

She mumbled, her face still hidden, 'It was all your fault. All those things you said about the two of us, pretending we were having an affair——'

'But you wanted to get rid of him. Roland told me.'

Her head came up. 'Get rid of him, yes. But you made him worse. He dragged me in here and—and assaulted me!'

He frowned. But when she said, with an unmistakable touch of pride, 'I slapped his face and he got mad and went home,' he grinned.

'So the little mouse turned tigress again! It's that deep-down aggression of yours. My word,' the anticipatory gleam of the hunter came into his eyes, 'some man's going to have to come to grips with that and tame it one day.'

She stood unsteadily. 'All the same,' she softened her tone and looked at him, 'thanks for trying to help me. It was true. I did want to get rid of him.'

His eyes, which were searching hers, seemed puzzled, and now it was his turn to try to decipher the wordless message passing between them.

His hands lifted to her face. He whispered, 'You're looking at me as though you want me to kiss you. Did you know that?'

She shook her head, waiting. His arms went round her, his mouth came down and the kiss he gave her touched a treasure chest of feeling inside her. It burst open and the contents spilled and she was responding to his lips like any other girl deeply in love. She clung to him, yielding, and in answer to her passion his hand moved and he held her more intimately than he had ever done before. She didn't recoil, she didn't back away as she would have done in the past. She gave herself up at last to the ecstasy of being touched by the man she loved, and the thought drifted through her mind, like wisps of cloud in a bright sky, 'If he holds me like this, he must—he must love *me*.'

But he raised his head, disentangled himself from her arms and put her away from him. 'Goodnight, Elise,' he said quietly, and went home.

She dropped, defeated, into a chair. She had tried to tell him she loved him, the message had been there in her lips and her arms, but he had chosen to ignore it. Into the depths of her misery there came a shaft of light, like the sun finding a break in a cloud-ridden sky. She was not cold. She had warmth and passion like any other woman, because in Lester's arms she had come to life. But the sunlight turned to shadow, and her brief happiness faded, when she remembered with humiliation the firmness and finality of his rejection.

CHAPTER X

ELISE asked her brother, a few days after the party, 'When Lester was away, do you know if he saw Nina?'

Roland lowered his book, showing impatience at being disturbed. 'Yes, he did. Why?'

She made her tone indifferent. 'I just wondered if they had got engaged again.'

'I can answer that straight away. They didn't.'

'How do you know?'

He sighed and put down his book, reconciled now to a long interruption. 'He told me that Nina had tried to see him—you know she lives next door to his parents?—but he refused. In the end, his mother persuaded him to agree to see her and apparently Nina pleaded with him to let them carry on from where they'd left off.'

He paused and she whispered, 'What then?'

'Lester said "no". At which point it seems, she burst into tears and cried all over him, but he still wasn't having any.

His mother argued with him and tried to make him change his mind. Then Nina's mother had a go.' He laughed. 'One big happy family party.'

'Then what?'

'Nothing. He was adamant. Said he'd finished with women, Full stop.'

She moistened her lips. 'Was that why he came back early?'

'Yes. He couldn't stand the fuss. Now apparently she keeps pestering him by phoning him every other day. He tries to put her off and is quite rude to her, but it seems to make no difference. She won't give in.'

He turned the pages, trying to find his place. 'Whether or not she'll wear him down and make him change his mind remains to be seen. Personally I doubt it.'

'So he really meant what he said,' she murmured, after a while, 'he really has put women out of his life.'

'So it seems.'

Their father came in. He tutted, having heard what they were saying. 'Are you talking about Lester again?' He listened while Elise repeated what Roland had said.

Harold laughed. 'You're not telling me that a good-looking young fellow like that is going to be allowed to escape from the bonds of matrimony for the rest of his life, when the world is full of designing females?'

Elise knew he was being facetious but she insisted, 'He is, Dad. He's absolutely determined.'

But Harold was not convinced. 'Don't you believe it. Shall I tell you what I think? I think he's met someone else he likes better.'

Her heart began to race. 'But, Dad, he's not friendly with any other girl.'

Roland lowered his book. 'She's right. I know for certain he hasn't got a girl-friend.'

'You can argue as much as you like, both of you, but take it from me—and I've got more experience of human nature than you have—he's got a secret love, a woman tucked away somewhere.'

She wanted to cry out, 'You're wrong, it's not true, there isn't a woman in his life.' But she stayed silent and kept her misery and doubt to herself.

Towards the end of the following week, Elise had finished her shopping and was waiting for the bus. She was heavily laden and tired. She was also depressed. Since the night of the party, Lester had not been near the house. She had spent hours trying to think of a reason for his continued absence. Even Roland seemed puzzled.

When she saw his car approaching, her heart throbbed at the prospect of being given a lift home, of sitting beside him and talking to him again. It was not until he was almost level with the bus queue that she realised he would not stop. He had not even seen her. And no wonder—there was a girl sitting in the passenger seat and Elise knew at once who she was.

So Nina had worked the miracle, achieved her object—she had worn his resistance down and they were back together again. She had, it seemed, achieved the impossible. In the face of her persistence, he must have given in and invited her to stay with him.

In the bus, on the way home, Elise stared miserably out of the window. The photograph had done the girl justice. From the brief glimpse she had had of her, Nina seemed to be as attractive in reality as the picture had suggested. Lester had probably pretended to refuse to take her back merely to salve his pride. That done, he had obviously relented and agreed to become engaged to her again.

As she let herself into the house, Elise told herself she could not blame him. What man would continue to say 'no' to such a beautiful girl?

When the telephone rang during the evening, she was in no hurry to answer it. She knew it would not be Lester.

It was, in fact, Howard. He mumbled something about being sorry for what had happened at the party and would she agree to go out with him again? 'I'd like to see you, Elise. I promise to behave better next time.'

He sounded surprisingly apologetic, but his desire to appease did not flatter her, nor did it make her any more eager to see him again. She started to refuse, but checked herself. Why shouldn't she go out with him?

Perhaps Lester was right. It would be foolish to turn down such an opportunity—marriage to a stable, solid, decent-living man who could offer her every comfort. The only demands she would find it difficult to meet would be those which any husband would make of his wife. And even those, she told herself, grimly, she would no doubt accustom herself to in time.

'All right, Howard, I'll go out with you.'

He seemed sincere in his thanks and they arranged a time. As she put the receiver back on its cradle, the doorbell rang.

'Hallo, Elise,' Lester said, his hand on the arm of the girl at his side.

'Hallo, Lester,' she answered, her face blank.

Nina smiled at her, her eyes bright in anticipation of the welcome she was sure she would receive from Lester's friends. Lester introduced the two girls.

'Elise,' his hand motioned them towards each other, 'Nina, my ex-fiancée.'

Nina flashed him a smile. 'Not so much of the "ex", darling.'

Her eyes became coolly estimating, taking in the dowdy clothes Elise was wearing, the face free of make-up, the uncombed hair. 'Isn't Elise the girl, Lester, you described on the phone that day as "stunning"?' She laughed gaily. 'Do you know at the time, I really thought you meant it!'

'Did you?' His face held no expression. 'Now you can

170

see for yourself that I was joking, can't you?'

Elise took them into the sitting-room. 'Where's Roland, Elise?' Lester asked shortly. 'In his room?'

He was up the stairs before she could reply.

'What a pleasant house,' Nina said, looking round.

'It needs redecorating,' Elise replied, trying to keep the sharpness from her voice.

'It—er—it's not exactly what you would call modern, though, is it?' Nina commented casually. 'Although I expect it's solidly built.'

'Very,' said Elise, frowning and turning her face away so that the other girl could not see it. Did she have to be so condescending about everything? Did Lester know what he was doing? Beauty or no beauty, the girl's personality hardly seemed to fit in with his down-to-earth cynicism.

'Lester and I,' Nina was saying, 'have been looking round the houses on the estate he's building. I think they're beautiful, and so well designed. With any luck, one of them should be ready in time.'

'In time for what?' Elise wanted to ask. 'Our wedding,' would have been the answer, and they were two words she did not want to hear.

'Would you like a cup of tea?' she asked, her tone drained of life.

Nina patted her middle. 'Oh dear me, no, thank you. We had such a lovely meal at Lester's place. Mrs. Dennis is a darling and such a good cook, don't you think?'

'I really don't know,' said Elise, 'I've never had the chance to find out.'

Nina laughed and her expression became distinctly gloating. 'Of course,' it seemed to say, 'you aren't Lester's wife-to-be. You are not as privileged as I am.'

She sank back against the cushions and waited patiently for the return of her fiancé. She did not have long to wait.

Roland followed Lester down the stairs. The introductions were performed and Roland said, 'Lester tells me you're on holiday, Nina. I expect you're going to make the most of your few days away from the hospital.'

Elise frowned at her brother. Need he be so nauseatingly polite?

'I certainly am.' She smiled at Lester. 'I've been worked off my feet in the wards lately. Now I'm looking forward to being taken round and having fun before I go back into the maelstrom. Aren't I, darling?'

'Yes,' said Lester vaguely, 'I suppose you are. Unfortunately, my spare time is limited, but I'll see what I can do.'

Nina slipped her arm possessively into his and gazed up at him. 'Now there's a wonderful fiancé to have.' She turned to Elise. 'Have you got a boy-friend?' Her eyes skated disparagingly over her as if anticipating a negative answer.

'Yes,' Elise said, feeling a thrust of pleasure at Nina's surprise, then turning her eyes defiantly to Lester. 'His name's Howard.'

Lester bristled like a snarling dog, then his lips curled cynically. 'So you've made it up?'

She avoided his eyes. 'I'm going out with him tomorrow.'

Nina laughed happily. 'Just like us, Lester. We've made it up, too, haven't we, darling?'

He didn't bother to answer. It was so obvious that they had.

'Come on, Nina.' He urged her towards the door.

As they drove away, Harold arrived home. 'Who was that gorgeous vision in Lester's car?'

'Nina,' said Roland, 'his ex-fiancée.'

' "Not so much of the 'ex', darling," ' Elise mimicked in Nina's silvery tones. She went on sourly, 'She's been restored to full "fiancée" status. On her own terms, too, judging by the way Lester is pandering to her every whim.'

'You surprise me,' said Harold. 'That's hardly in charac-

172

ter. He doesn't strike me as being a man to pander to any woman's whim.'

'You're not always right about people, Dad,' Elise said wearily, going up the stairs.

'That's what you think, young lady,' he muttered to himself, as he shut his bedroom door.

Later, the telephone rang. Roland answered. 'Elise,' he called, 'it's Lester. He wants to talk to you, not me.'

'Yes?' she said into the mouthpiece, her voice dragging with tiredness.

'Is it true what you said about going out with Howard?'

'Of course. Why shouldn't I go out with him?'

'After all you've said about him, and after sending him packing the other night?'

'I've changed my mind. I'm entitled to, aren't I?'

'Being a woman,' he snapped back, 'and a particularly stupid one at that, of course you are. But it can only mean one thing—that you've decided to marry him after all.'

'Well,' she shouted, tears welling out of her eyes, 'you've changed your mind about Nina, you're going to marry her, so——'

She heard what sounded like 'damn Nina' but she knew she must have been wrong. After all, the girl was probably standing beside him, holding his hand.

'There's no need to shout,' he reprimanded. 'I'm not deaf.'

'You may not be deaf, Lester Kings,' she wanted to cry out, 'but you're blind, blind, blind . . .'

'All right,' Lester snarled, 'make a complete mess of your life. Marry him. Enjoy his worldly goods. *And* his love-making!' The receiver was slammed down and there was silence.

She went out with Howard. She even tolerated his kisses, managing by a great effort of will to appear as though she was responding. He seemed satisfied with the evening's achievements.

'We'll get a ring.' He looked at her. 'Shall we?'

She knew he was testing her, getting at last a definite answer to his proposal of marriage.

'Yes,' she said, keeping her eyes down and steeling herself for the passionate kiss which she knew would follow her acceptance. With rigid self-control she managed not to recoil as his lips fastened hungrily on hers.

She closed her eyes. The bulldozer was upon her, levelling her to the ground, grinding her emotions into the dust and carrying away with it her last shreds of control over her own destiny. Howard had won.

He took her home. 'When shall we get the ring? Next week?'

Why not? she asked herself. There was no reason now for delay.

'Next week,' she promised, getting out of the car.

When Elise arrived at the shop the following morning, Phil Pollard was in the office. Clare beckoned to her, made a face and whispered, 'He's a bit sour. Watch your step.'

It was so unusual for Phil to be ill-tempered that Elise felt nervous as she opened the office door. He turned as soon as she entered.

'Good morning, Mr. Pollard.' Her voice sounded overbright.

He nodded abruptly and went on flicking through a batch of invoices on his desk. She removed the cover of the typewriter and sat down. The silence was unnerving and she began to feel guilty for no reason at all.

'So you won't be working here much longer.'

It was spoken so sharply and so irritably she rotated on her chair and stared at him. He surely couldn't have heard about her engagement to Howard because she hadn't even told her family yet.

She asked him what he meant.

He looked at his desk. 'I've heard rumours...'

174

'What about?'

'I bought something at Wilf Frenley's yesterday and he told me about you and——'

She broke in, 'Lester Kings?' Her laugh dismissed the subject as though it were too trivial to discuss. 'Yes, I've heard it myself, but there's no truth in it at all.'

He was not listening. 'After pretending to be on my side, even joining in the protests, how you can go over to the enemy to the extent of having an affair with him——' He shook his head. 'You, of all people—I simply can't understand it.'

'But, Mr. Pollard, it's not true!'

He looked at her then, and caught the earnestness in her face, the sincerity in her tone and seemed to begin to believe her. But his expression became stubborn and mistrust seeped back into his eyes. She had failed to convince him.

Hoping at least to appease him she asked, 'Have you been to the estate lately? Have you seen how artistically the whole development has been planned?'

He growled, 'Been up there? I almost live up there. I haunt the place. I tell myself I'm mad to go, because it hurts every time I think of how it should be looking, now, in the spring . . .'

She turned back to her work. She was wasting her time trying to convince him. His words came back to her—'I haunt the place.' She held her breath. Was Lester right? Was Phil Pollard taking his revenge against the Kings family? Was he engaged in a cold-blooded campaign of retribution?

But she could not believe that he was capable of it. It was surely not in his nature, his honest, upright nature—was it?

That evening the storm broke. Elise was as usual in her room. Her father was working, Roland was getting ready to go out with Clare. The house was silent. The record she had chosen to listen to was *Schéhérezade*. But this time its

175

magic was not working.

She was restless, worried, tortured by a premonition of impending trouble. As she removed the headphones, impatient with herself, the doorbell pealed. It didn't ring, it pealed and went on and on until it was answered. She heard the familiar, ominous words, 'Where's your sister?'

She knew the voice and she knew the tone. It frightened her. She heard the heavy booted footsteps pounding up the stairs. The door was flung open and Lester burst in. He was wearing working clothes, so he must have come straight from the building site. He was beside himself with anger.

He strode across to the bed, his hands came out and he gripped her shoulders. He shook her mercilessly, the pressure of his fingers bruising her flesh.

'Will you call off your gang? Will you call off your vandals? You've made your point. You'll never forgive us for building on those damned woods.' He gave her a last violent shake and took his hands away. Her head sagged to her chest. 'All right, I've got the message,' he thundered. 'You hate my guts and my grandfather's. Now bring this dangerous nonsense to an end!'

Dazed, her head throbbing, she raised wild, frightened eyes and stared at him. The words came hoarsely, 'I don't know what you mean.'

He bent over her, his expression menacing. '*I don't know what you mean*,' he mimicked cruelly. 'I'll tell you what I mean. I mean that the house that was almost completed, the one we had decorated and furnished and were intending to open as a show house,' he paused, as a thought struck him, 'the house, in fact, you were inspecting so thoroughly the day the dog attacked you——'

She whispered, 'The house where the hornbeam stood?'

'The *very* one. The one you would have most reason to resent.' He paused. 'I see you know all about it. Do I need to go on?'

She mouthed the word 'Please.'

176

'That house is now windowless—every single one having been systematically smashed. Paint—taken with magnificent irony from the paint store—has been flung over the walls in every room. The kitchen fitments have been wrenched out and smashed, most of the furniture hacked to pieced. *Now* need I go on?'

Her hands were pressing against her cheeks, her eyes wide with fear as she remembered—'*I haunt the place,*' Phil had said. 'I'm sorry, Lester,' she managed to whisper, 'I know nothing about it.'

'Oh, drop your injured innocence act. I know you're involved, despite the fact that you've taken up with Howard Beale again—probably to act as a cover. Stop trying to shield Phil Pollard. He's the culprit, isn't he? With the gang of louts he's recruited locally, he's the one at the bottom of it. With your devoted, loving support.'

She looked bewildered. 'My *loving* support?'

'Don't look so pure and artless, trying to pretend there's nothing going on between you, when I know damned well——'

She clapped her hands over her ears. '*Stop it!*' She wanted to scream with laughter at the irony of it all. That morning Phil had accused her of a liaison with Lester. Now Lester was accusing her of the same thing with Phil.

He took her cry as an admission of involvement. He went on in a quieter tone, 'This is a police job now, Elise. I've put if off because of——' He stopped, but she knew what the missing word would have been. He continued, 'Because of the publicity which would necessarily follow. Now it's different. I'm sorry, Elise, but I'm calling them in.'

She looked at him imploringly. If she could persuade him to delay calling the police just a little longer, she could talk to Phil, beg him to stop, perhaps make him realise the futility of his actions.

'Please, Lester, please wait,' she whispered, 'just a few more days.' But she saw from the hardness in his eyes that she was pleading in vain.

There was both pity and disgust in the look he turned on her. 'Are you so infatuated with the man that you would even try to prevent me from taking the perfectly justifiable step of seeking police help in putting a stop to his criminal activities?'

She stood up. 'It's not Phil, Lester, I swear it's not Phil!' She caught at his arm to make him listen, but he shook her off savagely. He went out, down the stairs and out of the house.

Her father stood in the doorway. Roland joined him. 'What was all that about?'

She sank down on to the bed, staring at them without seeing them. 'It was Lester. He—he——' She could not go on. She threw herself face down on the bed, clawing at her pillow and crying with hopelessness and defeat.

The two men looked at her prostrate body, heard her gasping, hysterical sobs. Shocked and astonished, they stared at each other, silently asking the same incredible question.

Phil was away from the shop next day. Elise did not dare to wonder why. She was depressed and quiet, and now and then caught Clare's puzzled look. But Clare asked no questions, probably guessing that if she had done so, Elise would have burst into tears. The morning crawled by. At the back of Elise's mind was an intolerable fear. Every time the shop bell rang, she wondered, 'Is it the police?' Every time she heard Clare talking to a customer, she wondered, 'Is that a policeman come to question me?'

It was lunchtime and still no one had come to take her away. She asked Clare, 'Would you like me to help in the shop this afternoon?'

'No, love, I'll manage on my own. You go home and have a good rest. You'll feel better tomorrow.'

But Elise could not rest. She tackled the housework, hoping it would provide an outlet for her anxiety. But it didn't work out that way. All the afternoon she found herself straining her ears for the dreaded telephone call, the ring at the door which would announce the arrival of the police. It didn't occur to her that if they had come, her innocence would soon have been established as a result of their questioning. Because Lester thought her guilty, she felt herself to be guilty.

She was alone that evening. Roland had gone to Clare's and her father was taking an evening class at the technical college. She stood at the window, weary with a tense sort of tiredness, restive with a disturbing urgency that would not let her be. She watched the rain soaking into the earth and shivered, feeling a chill in the late April air. It was twilight and the clouds hung low and menacing, making the sky prematurely dark.

She could not stay in the house alone, with nothing to do but fight her fears. She would exorcise this ghost of guilt, she would go to the building site. She ran upstairs and put on her new red jacket and trousers, drawing on her boots and tucking the trouser legs into them. She tied the strings of her hood tightly under her chin and went out.

Why, she asked herself as she splashed through puddles and tested with her tongue the raindrops that settled on her lips, why had she come out on such a night? The rain was a soaking curtain of water, the air steamy with a hint of mist. Passers-by glanced at her with interest, admiring the colour of her outfit and the firmness of her tread.

By the time she reached the entrance to the estate, she had given up trying to find a reason for her sudden decision to go there. Perhaps it had been instinct, or feminine intuition, but whatever the reason, the fact remained that the place was beckoning her on like a crafty, knowing finger.

She stopped to listen. Nothing moved except her breath in the still, damp air. There was a waiting all around, an uncanny stifling silence that oppressed and troubled her.

The stillness made her furtive and she looked about her covertly, remembering the last time she had walked in the woods, just before the trees had been felled.

Her imagination played tricks and she peopled the place, not with human beings, but with the trees themselves come back to life, ghostly shadows returned to reclaim the earth that had been their for hundreds of years. In reality they had gone, but their spirits were all around, haunting the houses that had usurped their rightful places in the soil.

There was a creeping coldness on her skin. A prickle of fear roughed up her hair and scratched like thorns over her scalp. Like a monument to things past, the house built where the hornbeam had stood towered in front of her, the house that had been desecrated by someone with a vicious desire for revenge.

She looked through the windows and recoiled at the devastation inside. Whoever had caused that destruction was a person to be shunned and feared. She turned away, suppressing a shudder, unable to bear the sight of it. There was no light or sign of life in the site office, so Lester was not there.

But something caught her eye and she froze with terror. There was a movement, a muffled noise. Or was it the effect of the half-light in the rain-soaked silence? She peered at the outline of the site office, straining her eyes to penetrate the grey curtain of rain. She caught her breath and held it. Someone *was* there—a man—and he was trying to break in!

There was a tinkle of glass and she started to run towards the sound. Instinct, unthinking and foolhardy had prompted the action, and it was only when she was within talking distance of the intruder that she realised her mistake. Instead of running into danger, she should have gone for help. Now it was too late.

CHAPTER XI

SHE pulled herself up sharply, intending to turn and make for the roadway. But the man had seen her.

He dropped down from his perch on the hut windowsill and came towards her, his head slightly down, collar up, a dirty red scarf tied round his neck. His malevolent eyes ravaged her. As he thrust his grinning face up to hers, she knew at once who it was.

'So you're the one,' she whispered, 'who's doing all the damage, stealing all the things ...'

'Clever, aren't you?' he snarled. 'And you're the bird who got me fired that day.' She backed away, but he went after her. 'I owe you something for that, sweetheart.' He glanced round slyly. 'We're all alone. No one to interrupt. I'll settle my debt with you—*right now*!'

He leaped upon her, locked his arms round her and forced her back and down to the ground. She hit the earth with a stunning thud. She shrieked and struggled, trying to wrench herself free, using her nails, her feet and her voice. '*Lester*!' she screamed. '*Lest—er*!'

But Lester was not there to hear her call.

A hand hit her mouth and stayed there and she bit into the flesh with the strength and ferocity of an animal. He shouted with pain, but his grip on her body did not lessen. His hands were making their slow, relentless, murderous way towards her throat.

There came a snarl and a savage growl. Four legs and a body covered with mud-matted fur leapt upon the man's back. Teeth, sharp and vicious, fastened on to his jacket and pulled and tugged and tore and twisted, and penetrated to the skin.

Terror-stricken, the man rolled away, giving Elise her freedom. She scrambled up, holding her breath, watching with fascinated horror as the dog attacked the man as the man had attacked her.

With a superhuman effort born of a desire to survive, the man succeeded in heaving himself upright and on to his feet. Then he ran for his life over the rubble and across the fields, with the dog at his heels, snapping and howling and yelping in merciless, unrelenting pursuit.

The shouting, the snarling and the pounding footsteps grew fainter and died away. She was alone again in the quiet eerieness of the rain-soaked night. Only her heavy breathing disturbed the stillness, mingling with the hiss of the rain as it encountered the saturated earth and rebounded off the bricks and timber and grey tarpaulins.

She looked down at herself, holding her arms wide as if afraid of becoming contaminated with the filth that caked her clothes. Her limbs were shaking, her teeth were chattering uncontrollably, and as her brain began to extricate itself from the mire of her tangled emotions, she wondered what to do.

'Lester,' she thought, 'I must tell Lester.' She turned herself round, stiff as a walking doll, and with slow mud-hindered steps picked her way across the rubble to the road.

It took her longer than she anticipated to get to Alfred Kings' house, but every time her footsteps faltered, she thought of Lester and steadied herself. As she dragged along the garden path the front door seemed as distant as the gateway to Paradise. Her finger groped towards the bell, made contact and pressed it. The firm decisive footsteps which responded to the ring were the sweetest sound she had ever heard.

'Oh, my dearie,' said an anxious, compassionate voice, enveloping her with warmth even before she stepped into the hall. 'Come in, come in, do.'

Elise stood, bedraggled and helpless, on the front door mat. She heard Mrs. Dennis call, 'Mr. Lester, Mr. Lester, come quick!'

Upstairs a door opened. A voice answered, 'Something wrong Mrs. Dennis?' Lester leaned over the banisters. 'Elise!' He raced down the stairs. 'My God, what happened to you? *Tell me what happened!*'

But she shook her head, unable to speak, lifting her hands in an appealing, hopeless gesture. His arms came out and she went into them. Regardless of her plight, they closed round her, gripping her to still her shaking body.

'Now tell me,' he urged, his voice rough, 'tell me what happened.'

She mumbled against his chest, 'A man—he was breaking into the site office. I disturbed him and he—he attacked me. I think—I think he was going to strangle me.'

'Oh, dearie me,' moaned Mrs. Dennis.

'What man?' He lifted her chin, making her eyes meet his. 'What man, Elise? Tell me the truth. Was it Phil Pollard?'

'No,' she whispered, 'it wasn't Phil Pollard. But I recognised him. I can't remember his name, but it was the one you dismissed that day I was there.'

'You mean Wayman, who molested you?'

She nodded. 'He's the one who's been doing all the damage. He as good as admitted it.' She told him haltingly how the man had knocked her to the ground and started assaulting her, and how the Alsatian, the dog that had once attacked her—had appeared from nowhere and come to her rescue.

'And he drove Wayman off? Good for him! Where's Wayman now?'

He laughed grimly when she told him that the last she had seen of him was when he was running for his life across the fields with the dog baying at his heels.

'Oh, the poor young lady,' Mrs. Dennis moaned again. 'Let's get those wet things off her, Mr. Lester. She'll catch her death of cold.'

He held her away from him, untying her hood and un-

183

zipping her jacket. She stood, unresisting as a child as he peeled it off and handed it to Mrs. Dennis.

'They're ruined, Lester!' Elise wailed, revealing unconsciously how much she prized the clothes he had bought her, 'and you gave them to me.'

'Never mind, love,' he said, like a father soothing a distracted child, 'I'll buy you some more.'

'The trousers, Mr. Lester?' Mrs. Dennis asked.

'They don't matter,' Elise mumbled.

But Lester said, 'Would you wear a pair of mine, Elise? We could secure them round the waist with a belt and turn them up at the ankles, are you game?' She nodded and he smiled. 'It's a good thing clothes are "unisex" these days! Mrs. Dennis,' he turned to the housekeeper, 'my blue velvet cords? Could you get them?'

She bustled away. He took Elise's hand and led her towards the lounge. He switched on the light, but she stopped at the door.

'My boots are too muddy. Mrs. Dennis will——'

'Mrs. Dennis won't. Sit on the couch.' He lifted her feet one by one and tugged at the boots. Mrs. Dennis puffed in, flushed with exertion, and handed over the trousers.

'Get into these, Elise, while I phone the police. Mrs. Dennis will help you.' He went out.

The housekeeper pulled the curtains across the windows and picked up the boots and the mud-stained slacks Elise had dropped to the floor. Lester's trousers were much too long, but the wide leather belt kept them in place. Mrs. Dennis knelt down and turned them up clear of the floor.

'I expect you can squeeze into my slippers, dearie,' she said.

'Please don't trouble, Mrs. Dennis.'

'Trouble, indeed! It's no trouble after what you've been through. I'll get them.'

Elise sat in the silent room and closed her eyes, listening to Lester talking to the police. He was giving them a detailed description of the man who had attacked her. When he came in, he handed her a pair of pink fur-lined slippers.

'With Mrs. Dennis's love.' He helped her put them on. 'And get into this. It's mine. It should at least stop your teeth chattering like a couple of typewriters!'

She pulled the thick white cable stitch sweater over her head and revelled in its warmth. It was too large and they laughed at the sleeves hanging down over her hands. Lester turned them back over her wrists. 'Now sit down,' he said with a gentle push, making her do as she was told.

She leaned back, white-faced and still in a state of shock. 'I'm sorry, Lester,' she whispered, 'to give you all this trouble——'

'Will you be quiet!' Her eyes came open at the roughness of his tone. 'If I could lay my hands on that—that brute——' He went to the sideboard. 'I'll get you a drink.'

'No, thanks, Lester.' She added a little shyly, 'But I'd love a cup of tea.'

'Of course.' He went to the door. 'Mrs. Dennis, any tea going?'

'Certainly, Mr. Lester,' her voice wafted from the kitchen, 'I'll make some straight away.'

He stood on the hearthrug looking down at her with a curious expression on his face, a mixture of compassion, indulgence—and something else she could not define. Pity, perhaps or—she winced at the thought—brotherly concern?

She said earnestly, wishing to exonerate an innocent man, 'You see, Lester, it wasn't Phil Pollard after all. I knew it wasn't.'

He walked the length of the room and back. 'No,' he said stiffly, 'as you say, it wasn't Phil Pollard. I hope he knows what an excellent advocate he has in you.' He got himself a drink and stared into the liquid. 'I'm sorry that I ever thought it was. I know how much you admire him——' he stopped abruptly.

She didn't enlighten him. She didn't say, 'He's nothing

to me, any more than Howard Beale is.' What was the use?
He wouldn't believe her.

He sat beside her and took her hand and her fingers responded by clinging to his. She took a breath to speak, to make conversation, but reaction and hopelessness caught up with her.

She whispered, her voice wavering, 'Lester, oh, Lester ...' She turned her head away to find comfort from a cushion, but he pulled her roughly against him and into his arms.

For a few blissful moments she lay there, serene and comforted, delighting in his nearness and his touch—until it came to her with a shock that by lying there in his arms she was letting him guess how much she loved him. And that was something she had vowed she would never allow herself to do.

She summoned the remnants of her energy and the last dregs of her resolve and started to struggle madly in her efforts to get away from him. When he realised what she was doing, he let her go.

He stood up, his eyes black with anger. 'What's the matter? Is there something about me that repels you? Is it because my name isn't Phil Pollard? Or even Howard Beale? Is that why, every time I approach you or touch you, you shrink from me as if I were contaminated with something unspeakable?'

She didn't answer. How could she tell him the truth? Hadn't he told her repeatedly by word and action how little she meant to him?

He said, as if goaded beyond endurance, 'I'm damned if I'm going to let a woman treat me with contempt. Especially the woman I love.' He caught her hand and jerked her to her feet and into his arms. 'You keep saying you hate me, but, by God, I'll make you love me! If it takes me the rest of my life, *I'll make you love me!*'

He took her mouth with his and his lips and hands were

186

as angry as his words had been. As her fuddled brain played his words back to her—that he loved her—she responded to his demands with joy and abandon. He was bringing her back to pulsating life, enticing from her the warmth and passion he craved and which, until that moment, she did not even know she possessed.

At last he held back from her and searched her eyes. 'It's true, Elise? It's not Phil Pollard or——'

'Or Howard Beale or anyone but you.'

'Since when, my love?'

She shrugged and laughed. 'Can't remember, it's so long ago. Since I bit you, probably.' She raised his hand and kissed the scar she had inflicted on him as a child. 'What about you?'

He smiled. 'Since I hit you, probably!' He put his lips to her head and kissed it where he had hurt her so many years ago.

They laughed, drunk with the discovery of their mutual love.

'But, Lester, why didn't you tell me?'

'I thought you were infatuated with Phil Pollard. I thought, quite wrongly, that that was why you were trying to shield him.'

'But when you kissed me on the night of the party, didn't you guess then?'

'My darling, I dared to let myself start hoping, then I told myself not to be a fool, because all you were seeking from me was comfort and reassurance after Howard's clumsy attempts to make love to you.'

'And I thought you loved Nina.'

'Not from the moment you came back into my life.'

'But you were so upset when she ended the engagement.'

He kissed her gently. 'Hurt pride, my love, nothing more.'

She drew away from him, remembering. 'You got engaged to her again. She told me.'

187

He pulled her back into his arms. 'Then she told you wrong. She wished herself on me last week. It was her holiday, she said, so I couldn't send her away, could I? But believe me, as soon as I decently could, I got her on the train back to Newcastle. Ask Mrs. Dennis.'

The lady in question opened the door, a laden tray in her hands. 'So that's how it is, is it? And very nice too!' They broke apart. 'Don't mind me,' she said, smiling broadly. 'Carry on. It's about time Mr. Lester got himself married, and to such a nice young lady!' She glanced doubtfully at the tray. 'You won't want this now, I suppose?'

'Of course we do, Mrs. Dennis.' Elise pulled herself with difficulty from Lester's arms and took the tray.

'Mrs. Dennis,' Lester whispered as she turned to go, 'don't tell my grandfather yet, will you? We'd like to be alone a bit longer.'

'Don't you worry, Mr. Lester, I won't say a word. He's fast asleep in the next room anyway!'

They drank the tea and ate the cakes and when they had finished, she said, 'Lester ...' He looked up expectantly. 'I did something—silly the day before yesterday.' She stopped.

He put his arm round her, smiling, and drew her close. 'Her first confession since we became engaged. This should be revealing.' He waited. 'Well, go on, darling. Having whetted my appetite, I can't wait to hear what terrible thing you did.'

She took courage from his indulgent tone, but kept her eyes down. 'I—got engaged to Howard.'

'You did *what*?' He shouted with laughter. 'That's the joke of the year! Elise Lennan, otherwise known as "little mouse", never had a boy-friend in her life before, gets herself engaged to two men at once!' He became serious. 'You'll certainly have to tell him. No, better still, let me have the pleasure. I said a long time ago "may the best man win".'

'And he did.' She kissed him, and he responded in good measure.

'Lester,' she studied the pattern on his tie as if trying to memorise every detail, 'I still can't understand why, if you really wanted me yourself, you introduced me to Howard.'

He made her look at him. 'So you still doubt me? I'll tell you why. Because I was a realist. I thought that if *you* didn't want *me*, I might as well do my best for you and provide you with a wealthy husband. Now wasn't that self-sacrificial of me! But when I saw him kissing you, and thought of him touching you and making love to you, my self-sacrifice turned into martyrdom, then into intolerable jealousy. I'm afraid I'm not made of the stuff martyrs are made of. But you must remember, Elise, that hardly a day passed when you didn't take apparent pleasure in informing me in one way or another that you hated me.'

'But, darling, I only said that because I loved you.'

He stared at her then clapped a hand to his head. 'For pity's sake! The idiocy, the twisted logic of a woman's mind! She loved me, so she told me she hated me! How the blazes was I to know that your interpretation of the verb "to love" was its exact opposite, "to hate"!'

She shook her head, unable to explain. She couldn't say, 'I was so afraid that if I had told you I loved you, I would have lost you for ever.' There were some things, she argued, you couldn't explain to a man and expect him to understand, not even the one you loved.

'Lester, where shall we live?'

'Where do you suggest?'

'Could it be——' dared she ask it?—'in the house where the hornbeam used to grow?'

He laughed and kissed her. 'I thought you'd say that. That house it shall be. I'll get it repaired and we'll have it redecorated to our own choice. We can choose the furniture and fittings together. Would you like that?' She nodded against him. 'I'll put a gang of men on to it tomorrow. As

189

far as I'm concerned, sweetheart,' he said softly, 'the sooner we can move into it, the better.'

There was another long silence, and when they pulled apart he said, 'By the way, darling, the police said they'll want a statement from you tomorrow. Will you be able to identify Wayman for them?'

'Easily.' She grinned. 'I bit him—on the hand. I'll be able to recognise my own teeth marks!'

Lester threw back his head against the cushions and laughed again. When he stopped, he said, 'I think you must spend half your life going round biting men.' He looked at his own scar. 'Have you marked him for life too?'

'Unfortunately, I doubt it. My teeth didn't get a hard enough grip!'

'You bloodthirsty little minx!' The phone rang and he pulled her behind him. 'Come with me to answer it. I daren't let the tigress out of my sight. She might go on the prowl looking for things to sink her fangs into!'

He answered the phone. 'Roland? Yes, I do know where your sister is. She's here. I've got her—for keeps. What do I mean? I mean we're getting married. No, I'm not drunk, I'm stone cold sober, as sober as any man can be who's just proposed and been accepted by the girl he loves. Thanks.'

He covered the mouthpiece and said, 'Roland sends his congratulations and says he and Clare are delighted.' He spoke to Roland again. 'There's a lot to tell you, which I can't repeat over the phone, but take it from me, your sister's had quite a day of it. Adventures unlimited. Incidentally, she tells me she's bitten another man.' He held the receiver to Elise's ear and she heard shouts of laughter. He said into the phone, 'She's two women in one, your sister, part mouse, part tigress. It will certainly make our married life interesting, because every evening when I get home from work I won't know which one will be waiting for me!' He laughed and listened, and turned to her. 'Your father's just heard the news. He's delighted and says he guessed your secret long ago. I wish he'd passed it on to me. It would have saved an awful lot of heartbreak!'

He returned to Roland. 'To tell you the truth, Roland, she's wearing the trousers—my trousers—already. She's certainly started as she means to go on! Yes, I'll bring her home safe and sound.' He replaced the receiver and held out his arms. She went into them.

He murmured against her hair, 'Now let's both begin as we mean to go on.' He kissed her lingeringly, took her into the lounge and closed the door.

Attention: Harlequin Collectors!

Collection Editions

of Harlequin Romances now available

We are proud to present a collection of the best-selling Harlequin Romances of recent years. This is a unique offer of 100 classics, lovingly reissued with beautifully designed new covers. No changes have been made to the original text. And the cost is only 75¢ each.

Not sold in stores, this series is available only from Harlequin Reader Service.

Send for FREE catalog!